Dragon Fever

Also From Donna Grant

Don't miss these other spellbinding novels!

REAPER SERIES
Dark Alpha's Claim
Dark Alpha's Embrace
Dark Alpha's Demand

DARK KING SERIES
Dark Heat (3 novella compilation)
Darkest Flame
Fire Rising
Burning Desire
Hot Blooded
Night's Blaze
Soul Scorched
Dragon King (novella)
Passion Ignites
Smoldering Hunger
Smoke And Fire
Dragon Fever(novella)

DARK WARRIOR SERIES
Midnight's Master
Midnight's Lover
Midnight's Seduction
Midnight's Warrior
Midnight's Kiss
Midnight's Captive
Midnight's Temptation
Midnight's Promise
Midnight's Surrender (novella)

DARK SWORD SERIES
Dangerous Highlander
Forbidden Highlander
Wicked Highlander
Untamed Highlander

Shadow Highlander
Darkest Highlander

ROGUES OF SCOTLAND SERIES
The Craving
The Hunger
The Tempted
The Seduced

CHIASSON SERIES
Wild Fever
Wild Dream
Wild Need
Wild Flame

LARUE SERIES
Moon Kissed
Moon Thrall

SHIELD SERIES
A Dark Guardian
A Kind of Magic
A Dark Seduction
A Forbidden Temptation
A Warrior's Heart

DRUIDS GLEN SERIES
Highland Mist
Highland Nights
Highland Dawn
Highland Fires
Highland Magic
Dragonfyre (connected)

SISTERS OF MAGIC TRILOGY
Shadow Magic
Echoes of Magic
Dangerous Magic

Dragon Fever
A Dark Kings Novella

By Donna Grant

1001 Dark Nights

EVIL EYE
CONCEPTS

Dragon Fever
A Dark Kings Novella
By Donna Grant

1001 Dark Nights
Copyright 2016 Donna Grant
ISBN: 978-1-942299-45-5

Foreword: Copyright 2014 M. J. Rose
Published by Evil Eye Concepts, Incorporated

Sign up for the 1001 Dark Nights Newsletter
and be entered to win a Tiffany Key necklace.
There's a contest every month!

Go to www.1001DarkNights.com to subscribe.

As a bonus, all subscribers will receive a free
1001 Dark Nights story
The First Night
by Lexi Blake & M.J. Rose

One Thousand and One Dark Nights

Once upon a time, in the future...

*I was a student fascinated with stories and learning.
I studied philosophy, poetry, history, the occult, and
the art and science of love and magic. I had a vast
library at my father's home and collected thousands
of volumes of fantastic tales.*

*I learned all about ancient races and bygone
times. About myths and legends and dreams of all
people through the millennium. And the more I read
the stronger my imagination grew until I discovered
that I was able to travel into the stories... to actually
become part of them.*

*I wish I could say that I listened to my teacher
and respected my gift, as I ought to have. If I had, I
would not be telling you this tale now.
But I was foolhardy and confused, showing off
with bravery.*

*One afternoon, curious about the myth of the
Arabian Nights, I traveled back to ancient Persia to
see for myself if it was true that every day Shahryar
(Persian: شهريار, "king") married a new virgin, and then
sent yesterday's wife to be beheaded. It was written
and I had read, that by the time he met Scheherazade,
the vizier's daughter, he'd killed one thousand
women.*

Something went wrong with my efforts. I arrived in the midst of the story and somehow exchanged places with Scheherazade – a phenomena that had never occurred before and that still to this day, I cannot explain.

Now I am trapped in that ancient past. I have taken on Scheherazade's life and the only way I can protect myself and stay alive is to do what she did to protect herself and stay alive.

Every night the King calls for me and listens as I spin tales. And when the evening ends and dawn breaks, I stop at a point that leaves him breathless and yearning for more. And so the King spares my life for one more day, so that he might hear the rest of my dark tale.

As soon as I finish a story... I begin a new one... like the one that you, dear reader, have before you now.

Prologue

London

January

The hot water splashed over Rachel's face as she stood beneath the spray. She braced her hand on the tiled wall of the shower and remained for a moment longer before she turned the faucet off.

Steam swirled around the bathroom as if alive, fogging the glass. She wiped off her face and body before wrapping the towel around her. The glass was cool against her palm when she pushed open the shower door and placed one foot on the mat. Then stilled.

Someone was in her hotel room.

Her gaze swung to the bathroom door she'd left cracked open. Her heart hammered against her ribs as her stomach clenched in fear. No one should've been able to get into her room. She'd bolted the door.

In an attempt to slow her racing heart, she took a deep breath. Then, slowly pushed open the door. She peered around the edge to find a man sitting casually in the overstuffed chair. Long black hair was pulled away and clasped at the base of his neck. Gold eyes watched her with a wealth of humor. And a smidgen of mockery.

She blew out a breath and leaned against the door of the bathroom as indifferently as she could while wrapped in a towel.

One side of his mouth lifted in a grin. "You don't seem surprised."

She took in his British accent that was a bit too perfect. Sam MacDonald was anything but what he said he was. It was a fact she accepted in order to get what she wanted.

His arms rested carelessly along the arms of the chair. One long leg was bent with an ankle resting atop his other knee. His white shirt was unbuttoned at his neck with no tie in sight. But that was usually the case.

There was something undeniably dangerous about Sam MacDonald. He frightened her, but it was men like him that gave her the information she needed to expose the truth to the world. So he was a necessary evil.

But that didn't mean she had to like him.

"How did you get in?" she demanded.

His smile widened, stretching his full lips but never reaching his gold eyes. "That's a secret I'll keep." Then he blinked, his chest expanding as he took in a breath, and his entire demeanor changed. "Get dressed. We need to talk."

She stepped back into the bathroom and closed the door with a sigh. She looked down at her hands to find them shaking.

"Stop it," she whispered to herself.

She had to get her nerves under control and quickly. Without delay, she dressed in a pair of black lounge pants and a loose-fitting, long-sleeved gray shirt. When she exited, Sam was in the same position. Except now there were two glasses of Scotch sitting on the coffee table.

Their gazes met. Rachel had learned to listen to her instincts, and as she looked into Sam's eyes, she saw determination, anticipation, and…a slow burning anger. He blinked, and the anger was gone, hidden once more.

It would show again. It always did. No matter how hard he tried, he couldn't hide it for long. She found it difficult to trust him because she knew he was keeping something from her.

"I don't like whisky," she replied as she walked from the bathroom. She tucked her leg beneath her and sat on the sofa opposite him.

He gave an indifferent shrug. "I'd advise you change your mind."

"Why?"

"You want to get close to one of the Dragon Kings, don't you?"

Her heart leapt, but she kept the emotion from her face. Finally! She'd been waiting for something on the Dragon Kings. It was about time Sam came through after he'd teased her with the information months ago.

That anger she kept seeing in his gold depths must have something to do with them. When it came to the Dragon Kings, her instincts told her what she saw in his eyes was the truth. It was the only reason she was working with him.

Then again, he'd done this to her before, tempting her with information on the Kings. She wasn't going to fall into that trap so easily this time. "I'm not in the mood for jokes."

Sam shot her a baleful look. "Do I look like the kind of man who jests?"

As a matter of fact, he didn't. He was more intense, and that said a lot. She still didn't reach for the whisky glass. "When? Where?"

"How many men ask you out in a week?"

She frowned and looked to the bathroom where she saw herself in the mirror. Her black hair was piled atop her head to keep it from getting wet. It wasn't straight or curly, but a frustrating mixture that did nothing.

Her lips were too thin, her skin too pale. She was too tall, and her face too square. Her only redeemable quality was her eyes.

Thanks to a continued—and exhaustive—interest in makeup, she'd mastered every look there was. Her skills allowed her to become whoever she needed to be, whenever she needed it.

"I get asked as often as I want," she replied coolly as she returned her gaze to him. "And I get left alone when I want."

He nodded his head of black hair. "You'll need to be sensual without looking like you're doing it on purpose."

"Not a problem. It's an easy look to pull off."

"You might find yourself attracted to him."

She cocked her head to the side as she looked Sam up and down. She recognized beauty and attractiveness. Sam was all that and more, and yet she felt absolutely nothing.

It was how she'd always been. She felt no attraction to men or women. Good looks began to matter less and less when she didn't feel any sort of desire.

For anyone.

"Not a problem."

He lifted a brow in question. "Do you find me attractive?"

"I think you're handsome, but I feel nothing."

His smile widened. "You're going to be perfect, Rachel."

"I want to expose the Dragon Kings. If you're not going to give me access to that, then don't waste my time."

"That's exactly what I'm giving you." He lowered his foot to the floor and scooted to the edge of the chair. "Go to the Hotel George V in Paris."

She raised her eyebrows at the super luxurious Four Seasons hotel, but what else did she expect from a Dragon King?

"A room will be waiting for you."

At this, she frowned. "The same hotel as him? That's not wise."

"You're a master of disguise with makeup. Use it to your advantage.

Everything you'll need to gain access to the *La Défense* exhibition centre will be waiting."

Now she understood. "The World Whisky Consortium."

"Dreagan never misses an appearance. They have the most sought after whisky in the world and headline the entire event all five days."

She would have days to study, photograph, and catch a Dragon King to expose him for who he was to the world. She could barely contain her excitement. It was always such a rush to reveal the true nature of an individual or company.

"The WWC is in two days." At least she wouldn't have long to wait.

Sam picked up something on the floor and tossed it on the coffee table next to their glasses of whisky. "There is information about your subject. Don't miss this chance."

"That won't happen." She took the file and opened it, expecting to see a photo of the target. Yet all that was included was a sketch. "No picture?"

"No."

She should've known there would be no explanation. "Who drew this?"

Sam reached for a glass and tossed back the Scotch in one swallow. Then he softly set it down and stood. "Don't let me down, Ms. Marek."

"When I come through with this, because I will, I want you to tell me who you really are."

He smiled while fastening the top button of his suit jacket. "Some things are best left secret."

She watched him walk from her hotel room in smooth strides. Only then did she take her glass of whisky and raise it to her nose, inhaling deeply. The first thing she noticed was the distinctive smell. It was irresistible, with a seamless blend of flavors she couldn't quite recognize.

The amber liquid passed her lips and touched her tongue before sliding down her throat. The richness of it caught her off guard. It had multiple layers that kept surprising her.

Another taste followed the first, and before she knew it, she had drunk it all. Rachel looked at the glass with aversion. She didn't want to like Dreagan whisky because it was made by the Dragon Kings—beings who didn't belong on Earth. But it was the only thing to do with the Kings that she did enjoy.

She replaced the glass and began to pack. There was much to do before her first meeting with her dragon target.

Chapter One

Two days later…

Paris

Asher fisted his hands that rested on his knees. He wasn't at all happy that Constantine had sent him to Paris. It wasn't that he minded pulling his weight at Dreagan. It was that he wished to drive himself.

He looked at the man hired to chauffeur him about the city with distaste. It wasn't the man's fault, but Con wasn't there for Asher to take it out on.

He looked out the window of the Jaguar XJ but didn't see the sights. His thoughts were on Dreagan and his brethren. He'd been gone a mere few days, but already Asher missed the Scottish Highlands that had been their home for millions of years. Yet the humans had no idea those who lived on—and ran—Dreagan Industries weren't human—but dragons.

Asher could still remember what France looked like before there was a Paris, or before there was ever even a France. The mortals claimed land as if it was their right, decimating it beyond repair while causing animals to go extinct or running them out of the very homes they'd had for eternity.

Much as the humans had done the dragons.

He clenched his teeth. Both the mortals and the Dragon Kings were to blame for that war and the deaths that were caused because of it. He blew out a breath loudly.

The driver looked at him through the rearview mirror. "Everything all right, *monsieur?*" the man asked with a heavy French accent.

Asher could speak French, but he replied in English. "Aye. I'm fine."

But he wasn't. None of the Dragon Kings were. In fact, they hadn't been good for some time. It wasn't just the Dark Fae who were trying to expose them to the humans—and doing a good fucking job of it.

It wasn't even the Light Fae who refused to side against the Dark and help the Kings.

It was the fact that a banished Dragon King was slowly, but surely, tearing their world apart.

Ulrik.

He was out of control. He killed mates of the Dragon Kings, attacked other Dragon Kings, partnered with Dark Fae and humans alike, all to one end—another war.

Asher didn't think Ulrik cared who the Kings fought as long as there was a war. But his main goal was the death of Constantine, King of Kings.

Con was far from perfect, but Asher certainly didn't want to be responsible for what was left of their race. He looked to the sky and wondered about his dragons.

He missed them so much that it threatened to swallow him whole. It was one of the reasons he'd sought his mountain for the last millennia.

But war had a way of changing things.

It caused the Kings to send their dragons across the dragon bridge to another realm to end the war with the mortals. War also caused them to lose many Kings in the Fae Wars.

Now the Dark Fae had taken things to a new level. They'd videoed the Kings in battle with the Dark and released it to the human world. That clip showed the Kings shifting back and forth from human to dragon.

The entire world was in an uproar wanting to know if Dreagan was truly the home of dragons. That kind of attention and surveillance had essentially grounded the Kings.

Where once they were limited in shifting and taking flight at night or during a storm, now they couldn't fly at all. Any shifting was done in their mountains, and then only if absolutely necessary.

With all that shite going on, Con wanted him to put on a smile and make nice at the World Whisky Consortium. When all Asher wanted to do was give everyone the finger before shifting and flying out.

His thoughts halted when they pulled up at the Hotel George V. He reached for the handle, but before he could grab it, the doorman had the door open.

Asher clenched his teeth in frustration and gave the man a stiff nod. Why did everyone insist on doing things for him? When he spotted another of the staff attempting to reach the hotel doors before him, he lengthened his strides and opened his own door.

Instead of letting out a *whoop* at beating the bellman, he smiled. The hotel was lavish luxury, and the very place the representative from Dreagan was expected to stay. But he'd rather something less…extravagant.

In minutes, he was being shown up to his penthouse suite. Asher tipped the bellman and waited for the door to close before he let out a breath. He looked around the living area with the pale floors, sea-foam green couch, and long, cream leather ottoman along with the white and gold chairs. Curtains in a dark golden color hung on either side of the expansive windows giving breathtaking views of Paris.

He walked into the dining area with the large, white rose floral-printed curtains. Then he bypassed the white chairs and table and headed straight to the liquor. With a drink of whisky—Dreagan, of course—in hand, he opened the balcony doors and walked outside into the cold to look at the Eiffel Tower.

He'd barely taken two drinks before there was a knock on his door. Asher answered it to find a petite woman in a burgundy business suit that hid any curves she might have. Despite her young age, she wore a severe expression that brought him up short.

Her lips flattened as she gazed at him behind wire-rimmed glasses. He tried to see the color of her eyes, but the reflection on her glasses prevented it. Black hair was pulled away from her face in a tight bun so he had no idea how long—or short—her hair was. With a black planner clutched against her chest, she pushed her way inside.

"I'm Ms. Engel, your assistant."

He watched her small frame march into the room. "I didna hire an assistant."

"Mr. Constantine did." She stopped in the middle of the living room and turned to him. "Every year for the past five, I've acted as Mr. Constantine's assistant. You're going to need my help."

Asher let the door close as he looked askance at the little drill sergeant. The last thing he wanted was someone dogging his steps while he was in Paris. It was bad enough he couldn't drive himself or open his own damn doors. Now this?

"What's your full name?" he asked. He was going to have to make the most of the situation.

"You can call me Ms. Engel."

He stopped before her. "I could, aye. But I asked for your name."

After several tense seconds where she debated on whether to tell him, she said, "Blossom Engel."

At first he thought she was joking. Then he realized that wasn't a possibility since Ms. Engel had probably never laughed a day in her life.

Blossom. Her name was Blossom. It was everything he could do not to even crack a smile. He wasn't hiding it well by the way her eyes narrowed at him.

"Well, Ms. Engel, where shall we start?" he asked, trying to see the color of her eyes again, but failing—again.

With a quick intake of breath, she flipped open the planner. "Tomorrow morning at seven your breakfast will be delivered to the room. As soon as you tell me your preferences, I'll notify the kitchen. At eight thirty, you have a meeting with a Mr. Hodges."

Asher sank onto the leather ottoman and rubbed his eyes with his thumb and forefinger as Blossom rattled on. There wasn't five minutes throughout the next day for him to have a thought to himself.

How the hell was he going to get through it all?

Chapter Two

Rachel stared at her computer screen, comparing the drawing she'd uploaded of the Dragon King to the man who strolled through the George V as if he owned it. Everyone rushed to do Asher's bidding without him even uttering a single word.

Just one more reason to hate the Dragon Kings.

Wasn't it bad enough that they were liars? Wasn't it enough that they set out to fool the world? The company would fall, along with every member of Dreagan. And she was the one who would do it.

She took in the tall form and the expensive dark blue custom-made suit, the cut emphasizing his wide shoulders and trim form. Asher walked with purpose, but softly, as if he were conscious of his feet striking the ground. His arms swung freely by his sides, but she saw no watch on either wrist. Those around him had to look up because he towered over them.

When her gaze finally reached his face, she took in the thick ebony hair cut short on the sides, but the top left longer. She was too far away to see the color of his eyes, but his gaze swept the lobby thrice while listening to a woman welcoming him.

Rachel knew the definition of beautiful. She recognized Asher's broad jaw that narrowed to his chin was considered handsome. Dark stubble highlighted his jaw and cheeks, giving him an air of daring sophistication.

Women of all ages at the hotel stopped and stared, the desire evident in the way they panted after him. She could acknowledge his good looks, but she never understood someone's ability to forget themselves while gawking at another.

Once he disappeared in the elevator, she returned to looking over the notes uploaded to the computer. As with anyone who came to WWC from Dreagan, last names were never used, so no one thought it odd.

There was a lot of *Mr. Asher this*, or *Mr. Asher that* being bandied around the lobby. Everyone at the hotel wanted to ensure he had the best experience possible. As if he would have any other kind staying in the penthouse.

She wished the file on him was larger. In fact, there wasn't much to go on other than the basics.

Name: Asher
King of: Hunter Greens
Tattoo: Left arm
Notes: Likes to be in charge. Rarely leaves Dreagan.

Everything else she would have to learn on her own. She expected him to show attention to at least one of the numerous pretty French women in the hotel, but it was like he didn't even see them.

She was going to have to rethink how she approached him. The alternate persona she created for her work as a journalist wasn't far from the real her. There would be a few slight changes, like colored contacts.

Fading into the background was her specialty. He would never know the times she followed him. With a little creativity, she was going to capture what no one else had. That leaked video would be nothing to what she would tell the world.

It infuriated her that Sam wouldn't tell her who had taken the video showing the Kings shifting, but he did confirm it was real.

That's what sold her on discovering more of the truth. It was time the world knew the facts about the men of Dreagan. Every human being on the planet deserved to know what kind of monsters walked among them.

Monsters who could shift, fly, and destroy by breathing fire.

Their wealth, business, and land had been obtained by secrets and lies. Every record she found had the minimum information on it. And many of those records had missing pages. So tracing the Dragon Kings was difficult. After two years of hard work, she was about to thwart whatever hidden agenda they had.

It helped that so much attention was already focused on Dreagan. More of that interest had followed Asher to Paris. All she had to do was wait for the perfect opportunity. Patience was something she'd acquired long ago, so she didn't mind waiting.

She closed her laptop and rose, making her way to the elevator. She was on the seventh floor, just one below the penthouse. On the ride up, she thought about the outfit she'd originally chosen for her first meeting with Asher. She decided the cream dress with the navy heels would work much better for a first impression.

Though Asher had been cordial and polite, he gave the appearance of wanting to be alone. She would have to gain his attention without blatantly doing so.

The elevator dinged as it reached her floor. She looked both ways as she exited before turning and walking to her door. After she entered her room, she strode past the living area to the bedroom.

It wasn't that she liked what she was able to do by applying a certain makeup method or acting a specific way, but it gave her ways into places and near people that other journalists couldn't.

Just last year she exposed the ugly truth about a water treatment plant in Oregon by getting close to the man in charge. In less than a month, he spilled all his secrets without her ever having to even take off her clothes.

Which is where she drew the line. She'd honed her interview skills as well as reading books on profiling and learning to read people's body language. If she couldn't get her information by questioning an individual, then she wasn't doing her job.

Some journalists did whatever it took for a story. Not Rachel. Then again, she found it difficult to even think about having sex with someone when she never felt any sort of passion. It didn't matter—man or woman—she was somehow lacking in that department.

As a teenager, it had terrified her. In her twenties, she thought she wasn't with the right men, so kept making changes. It wasn't until her thirties that she realized she was wired differently.

It wasn't that her body didn't have needs. It was that there wasn't a single person she'd run across in all her travels that made her heart race. She hadn't been consumed with lust.

With her…peculiarity…it allowed her to focus more on her work of exposing lies, corruption, or evil people to the world. It ensured she nearly always worked alone.

There was no making friends, because it was an inevitability that someone close to her would be affected by whatever she discovered and wrote about.

Her colleagues used to ask if she was lonely. What they didn't understand was that she preferred her solitude. She wanted to be on the outside looking in. There she saw the veracity of people and the world. The lies were harder to hide.

She opened her closet and pulled out the clothes, shoes, and clutch for the night. Then she went to her jewelry case. She only chose a few standard pieces that could be worn with anything.

Rachel lifted the lid and touched the pearl necklace that had been passed down from her grandmother before looking at the pearl studs that once belonged to her mother. When she saw the locket peeking out from beneath a small box, she sighed.

Her hand shook when she grabbed it. She let her thumb stroke the ivory rose amid the onyx before she pressed the button on the side. The locket popped open. Slowly, she opened it. Then she sank onto the bed and stared at the pictures inside.

* * * *

For three hours from his position on the sofa, Asher listened to Blossom Engel going on about meetings, dinners, tastings, and other such sordid affairs he would have to attend at the World Whisky Consortium.

"How the fuck does Con do this every year?" he mumbled.

Ms. Engel continued without hearing him. He'd already gone through half a bottle of Scotch. Right now, he was ready to fling himself over the balcony if Blossom didn't immediately vacate the premises.

"That's enough," he said over her.

She paused from her seat on the ottoman, lifting her brows as she gazed at him over the agenda book. "Sir? I don't think that's wise."

"I need tonight to myself."

"What you need is rest. The next few days are nonstop."

He briefly closed his eyes. "I know."

"I thi—"

"I think I'm going to strip out of these clothes and walk around naked," he interrupted.

There was a bit of hesitation, as if she were deciding whether to stay or not. After a few seconds, she cleared her throat. "As you wish."

He dropped his head in his hands. He couldn't help but smile as he wondered what the unflappable Blossom Engel would do if he shifted into a dragon right then. Knowing her, she would continue on as if nothing had happened.

It was no wonder Con used her.

"The hours of three to five on Friday have me a bit concerned," she said, a look of consternation crossing her brow. "I may need to shorten one meeting or move the other because of the overlap."

"Whatever you think." He got to his feet. "Ms. Engel, you're a delight, but I really need some time to myself."

"Just a few more minutes, sir."

"You said that an hour ago. Now, Blossom, we're going to be spending a lot of time together. Give me tonight."

Whether it was because he'd used her given name or that he left her no choice, she softly closed the agenda and stood. "I'll see you at eight thirty in the morning, sir," she said before exiting.

Asher released a long sigh and sank onto the couch. The quiet was just what he wanted. Thirty minutes later, it was too quiet.

He looked out the window at the lights coming on all over Paris as night fell. The longer he stood staring at the darkening sky, the more he wanted to feel the wind gliding over his scales as he soared with the clouds.

Irritation against the Dragon Kings' circumstances began to swirl. He realized how easy it was for other Kings to hold such hatred for the humans. After all, they had given up for their survival only to have the noose continue to tighten around them.

This was their planet. From the dawn of time dragons had roamed this world, ruling all. They could've easily killed the humans when they appeared, but they hadn't. The Kings had made room for them.

And where had that gotten the Kings?

Where once they ruled freely, they now hid.

Where once there were millions of dragons, there was now only the remaining Dragon Kings.

Where once magic pulsed liberally over the world, it was now confined to a few distinct places.

Where once the Kings could shift from dragon to human at will, even that had been taken from them completely.

Where once the Kings were regarded with respect and honor, they were now being hunted by every government, secret society, news outlet, and individual who sought the truth.

The truth. He snorted loudly. They wouldn't be able to handle the truth. It was why the Kings had gone to such lengths to keep the mortals in the dark.

He reached for the bottle of Dreagan whisky only to find it empty. Waiting for another bottle wasn't an option. Instead, he grabbed his jacket as he walked from the room.

When he reached the lobby and exited the elevator, he saw a man immediately come toward him. Asher held up his hand to stop him, giving the man a quick smile as he walked past.

He made his way to the bar. Most of the tables were occupied, as were the stools along the bar, but it wasn't so crowded that he felt he needed to leave. Though he'd never had a real issue with humans before, the current situation at Dreagan made the need for space a priority.

Then there was the fact he *ached*—deeply, voraciously—to shift. To hide who they truly were for extended periods was just...wrong.

Anger began to unfurl within him. But was that anger directed at the humans or the Dark Fae? Both were the cause of the Kings' state of affairs. Except, the blame could be placed on them. The Kings had a chance to wipe out the humans and the Dark—and had done neither.

So the fault lay with them.

Which didn't make him feel any better.

He'd just taken a stool when the bartender walked up. "Dreagan," Asher said.

"*Oui*," the bartender replied and hurried to pour the whisky.

He accepted the drink with a nod, keeping his hand around the glass as he surveyed the room. A table of two women was trying to get his attention. Asher learned it was better to ignore them rather than be polite. Women like those didn't take hints.

A group of five businessmen sat at a table alternatively discussing business and laughing at some joke while doing their best to gain the notice of the two women looking at him.

Then he saw her. She paused at the entrance of the bar, gazing about as if deciding to remain. Her long black hair fell in glossy waves over one shoulder and down her back. Her eyes briefly landed on him before she chose a table toward the back corner.

She had a confident walk that drew every male head her way—and a few females.

A cream dress molded elegantly to her curves, hitting two inches above her knee. A wide navy leather belt fit around her small waist and matched the heels. Large sapphire and gold earrings dangled from her lobes and matched the gold necklace and curved bar that sat at her neck.

She held a navy crocodile clutch in one hand while several gold bangle bracelets clinked around her wrist. On her left hand she had a slim gold thumb ring, and on her right she wore a wide gold filigree band around her middle finger.

With ease and elegance, she lowered herself into a chair and gave her order to a waitress. He put her square face to memory, from her high forehead to her perfect nose and wide lips. Her alabaster skin fairly glowed in the dim light of the bar. He followed her finger as she tucked her hair behind her ear.

That movement caused his balls to tightened. How something so mundane could cause such a reaction within him was startling—and exciting. He smiled when she politely declined an offer from one of the businessmen.

With a crook of his finger, he called the bartender over and sent a drink to the woman. He took a sip of the whisky and watched as the drink was delivered. When the waitress pointed him out, the woman's gaze slid to him. She gazed at him a long time before she smiled and motioned him to join her.

The night was suddenly looking up.

Chapter Three

It had been so easy to gain Asher's attention. Then again, she had dressed the part. Though Rachel hadn't expected such an immediate interaction with him, she was still pleased. She'd guessed right in what would draw his attention.

"Good evening," he said in a smooth, deep brogue that she wanted to hate but couldn't.

She nodded, smiling "Evening."

"Ah. American."

"Is that a problem?"

He was quick to shake his head. "No' at all. I've several close friends who are married to Americans. I'm Asher, by the way."

She took his hand. His long fingers tenderly wrapped around hers as his Scottish brogue fell from his lips. "Rae."

"A curiously male name for a verra feminine woman."

"It's a nickname." It was a trick of any good undercover journalist worth their salt to remain close to the truth in any scenario. Sharing an old nickname allowed her to use something other than her name, but still answer to it because she knew it.

"And your real name?"

She smiled flirtatiously. "That I save for those I deem worthy."

One side of his lips lifted in a shockingly seductive grin. He leaned back in his chair casually, those bright green eyes of his studying her, as if by staring he might be able to see all the secrets she kept hidden away.

Rachel found herself gazing into his eyes. Never had she seen eyes such a dazzling green before. Even if she hadn't known he was an immortal and a Dragon King, the truth of who he was blazed in those eyes of his.

"Your smile is fading. Why?" he asked, a small frown forming.

"Do you believe you can see a person's soul in their eyes?"

"Aye," he replied immediately.

She wasn't sure why she asked. She was supposed to flirt outrageously, not talk philosophy. But there was something in his green eyes that caught her off guard. It left her feeling…off balance. As if she couldn't quite catch her footing.

He set his whisky tumbler on the table, but kept his fingers around it. "What do you see in my eyes?"

She wanted to turn the conversation elsewhere, to lighten the mood and make him smile again. Instead, she fell deeper into his gaze. The clink of glasses, the laughter and conversation faded, leaving them in a cocoon.

He's dangerous, her mind warned. *He's a liar who needs to be exposed.*

Oddly, even her thoughts dwindled to barely a whisper. She tried to look away, but she was trapped, ensnared by eyes that watched her intently.

"Tell me, lass," he urged softly.

She suddenly understood the term "old soul," because one sat before her now. And, as if opening a book, she caught a glimpse of Asher. The words then tumbled out of her mouth. "Endlessness. Sorrow. Agony. Distress. Rage."

His head tilted to the side, surprise evident by the way his brows lifted slightly. She blinked and took a drink of her martini. She didn't like the way she felt off kilter, as if someone had pulled the rug from beneath her.

At this rate, she was going to ruin everything. He was supposed to be panting after her so much that he never noticed anyone else—especially when she was in her other persona—following him.

She quickly forgot about that as she reflected on her words. *Endlessness.* Was it the years he'd lived? Was immortality difficult to shoulder? *Sorrow. Agony. Distress. Rage.* What had hurt him so? Or was it a who? She suddenly wanted to know.

No! God, what was wrong with her? Why couldn't she keep focused on her mission? Her instincts were confused, as if they couldn't decide what to think.

"You saw quite a lot," Asher said.

She shrugged one shoulder. "You allow people to see what you want them to see."

"That's true of anyone."

"Why are you sad?" The question was out before she could stop it.

He briefly looked at his whisky glass and half-heartedly shrugged.

The seconds stretched by as silence lengthened. Finally, he said, "We all hold a wee bit of sadness, lass."

Wasn't that the truth? She should know. She'd been carrying around such sadness that it fairly weighed her down. "What is a Scotsman doing in Paris?" she asked to change the subject.

He turned the glass around with his fingers. "Business. You?"

"Does anyone really need a reason to come to Paris?" she asked with a grin. It was her attempt to lighten the mood.

"So you like the city?"

She gave him a wry look. "What's not to love? The amazing food, the magnificent museums, and the breathtaking sights."

"Do you come often?"

"Unfortunately, no. You?"

"First time in…a verra long time."

She understood that hesitation. It was on the tip of her tongue to ask him when the last time was, but she refrained. For now. "Are you going to take in all the sights?"

"If there's time."

"You should make time."

"Are you offering to show me around?"

Just what she'd been waiting for. She gave him her best seductive smile, angling her body so he could see her cleavage better. "I am."

"Then I'll have to make the time."

Despite her screw-up, she felt as if she'd made headway with Asher. He was going to be a tough nut to crack. He kept things close. He was untrusting, and she couldn't fault him for that. But she would get the truth. She was very good at her job, and everyone recognized her name on an article to mean it was truth.

For the next fifteen minutes, they talked of nothing and everything. She was surprised to find he had a love of reading that matched her own. Though he'd read all of the greats—Tolstoy, Faulkner, and Steinbeck—she was more than a little shocked to discover that he'd read—and enjoyed—Jane Austen and the Brontë sisters.

Listening to the way he spoke of his favorite authors such as J.R.R. Tolkien, Homer, Shakespeare, and F. Scott Fitzgerald, she saw another layer of the man. It didn't help her faltering instincts after looking into his eyes. That had been a mistake. One she wouldn't repeat with him.

Learning more about her subjects always happened when she had to get close to them. Sometimes it allowed her to see that they might have a smidgen of humanity within. Other times, it showed just how black their hearts truly were.

With Asher, she found it too easy to talk to him. Few men could keep up with her conversations regarding books she'd read and her thoughts. Not only did he know the authors, but he'd read the books.

Two hours later, she sat nibbling on a plate of cheese and croissants as she listened to him debate the finer points of *The Count of Monte Cristo*.

And the worst part was that she *agreed* with him!

It infuriated her. She couldn't soften toward him, no matter how enthralling she found his brain.

He finished his third Scotch and gave her that crooked smile. "Are you staying at this hotel?"

"I am," she replied and lifted the toothpick with the last olive to her lips. His gaze dropped to her mouth. She slowly wrapped her lips around the fruit and pulled it off the toothpick.

His face darkened with desire. A little thrill shot through her at being able to get such a reaction.

"Are you?" she asked softly.

His eyes slowly pulled away from her lips. "Am I what?"

"Staying here?" She inwardly smiled. Asher flustered. She liked that. *A lot.*

He gave a nod of his head. "I am."

"Isn't that convenient?"

He watched her for a few seconds silently, as if he wasn't sure what to make of her. "Verra. I have a dinner I can no' miss tomorrow, but if you're free, I'd like to meet you for drinks again."

"This was a pleasant few hours," she said as she got to her feet.

He rose as well. "Aye, lass, it was. Until tomorrow?"

Instead of replying, she smiled and walked around him. She didn't look back to see if he was watching, though she had to fight the urge. In all her years going undercover, none had engaged her mind while charming her—until Asher. It was an odd mix that she hated to admit she thoroughly enjoyed.

She didn't let down the persona of Rae until she was inside her room. With all the curtains drawn, she didn't have to worry about anyone seeing in. Still, she walked the entire suite to make sure she was alone.

Then she bolted the door and released a sigh. Her first meeting with Asher had gone better than she could've hoped. She'd expected to be the one continuing the conversation, as she normally had to do in such situations.

There had been a plethora of surprises that night. She wasn't sure if she was more amazed with Asher or her reaction to him.

If she did take him about the city, there was no doubt they would have fun. She nearly choked. When was the last time she had fun with someone?

It had been fifteen years. Such a long time to be on her own after losing her family. Since that time, Rachel found it easier to only make herself happy.

How…peculiar…to find that she hadn't wanted to leave him.

She twirled her thumb ring as she thought of all she'd seen while looking into his eyes. He hadn't contradicted what she'd seen. Unable to stop herself, she wondered what could make him feel such things.

He hadn't given her much of an answer. Her curious nature made it impossible for her to let something like that go. The answers wouldn't be found in her usual searches. Whatever she'd seen in his eyes was something deeply personal.

Rachel took off her shoes and placed them carefully in the closet before she removed the dress and put it on the hanger next to her other clothes. Only then did she slip on the robe and grab her laptop.

She watched the video of the dragons shifting a dozen times, seeking out any sight of a hunter green dragon. Since it was filmed at night, there was no way she could tell if Asher had been there or not.

Despite the fact she'd done extensive research on Dreagan, she did another search. Sam mentioned that there were many Dragon Kings living at Dreagan. That meant they had to interact with those in the local village.

She kicked herself for not thinking of this sooner, but there had been so much information on Dreagan Industries that it had taken up most of her time.

Sam had also provided her with specifics on Asher and Constantine. He wouldn't give her a list of all the Dragon Kings, which she found odd despite his claim of knowing who they all were.

She wasn't so naïve to trust blindly. Sam was using her, and since she wanted to expose Dreagan and the Dragon Kings, it worked to her advantage. But she was going to have to be careful with him.

A quick search brought up the quaint village where Dreagan was situated. With the tourism brought in from Dreagan, the town was beautiful and picturesque. It was a place she would want to visit.

As she scrolled through the website, there was mention of Dreagan everywhere. A list of "must visit" places took up the right-hand column. Right below Dreagan was a pub, The Fox and The Hound, which boasted some of the best drinks, food, and atmosphere in the area.

It was the article of the new medical office opening and the picture of a pretty redhead that caught her attention. A Dr. Sophie Martin, new to the area from Edinburgh and with a connection to Dreagan, had decided to open her own practice.

Rachel pulled up a new tab and did a search on the doctor. Another picture of Sophie pulled up. This one was inside a hospital, but she wasn't wearing a smile. More digging gave her Sophie's story, including a brief mention of a man connected to the doctor being relieved of his position.

No matter how much she looked, she couldn't find how Sophie was connected to Dreagan. If the Dragon Kings were all as handsome as Asher, it stood to reason that Sophie had a lover there.

But to quit her position in Edinburgh to open a small practice for a lover? No. It had to go deeper than that.

Rachel closed the laptop and leaned her head back on the sofa. There were two sides to every story. Not once since she began to show the world the corruption and immorality of companies or individuals had the other side of the story ever stopped her from doing her job.

No matter what she'd seen in Asher's eyes tonight, she wasn't going to stop. The world needed to know about the Dragon Kings and how dangerous they were with their abilities and immortality.

Chapter Four

Asher exited the car amid a flash of clicks from cameras as well as reporters doing their best to holler questions the loudest in the hopes he might answer.

"Is it true you're a dragon?" one reporter asked.

Another yelled, "Shift for us."

They had no idea how much he wanted to do just that, if for no other reason than to get everyone out of his face. Instead, he put on a serene expression, buttoned his jacket and gave a nod to a few spectators lined up along the entrance as he walked in.

Once inside the centre, there was no time to relax. Ms. Engel was right on his heels, directing where he was headed and giving him names of those he would be meeting.

He stopped outside of the closed doors of the room.

"Is something wrong, sir?" Ms. Engel asked.

"For one, my name is Asher, not sir."

She held up a finger to stop him. "Mr. Constantine also tried to tell me the same thing. I work for Dreagan and whoever represents the company at the WWC. While here, you'll always be 'sir.'"

Asher could accept that. Blossom was beginning to grow on him. She might be a miniature drill sergeant, but she was damn good at her job. No wonder Con used her year after year.

He drew in a breath and released it as he looked behind them. "Is it always so..." He waved his hand around, looking for the right word.

"Crazy? Insane? Nearly fanatical?"

He nodded. "Yes."

"Only when Dreagan is here." Ms. Engel put the cap on her pen. "Before TVL, everyone just wanted a glimpse of those who were a part of Dreagan and get a taste of the whisky. After TVL, well, now they want to see what might happen."

"TVL?" he asked, sorting through all sorts of words she might mean.

"The Video Leak."

"Ah." Well, that made sense. He turned his attention to her. "Did you see the video?"

"Of course."

When she said nothing further, he asked, "What did you think?"

"It doesn't matter, sir."

With that prim British accent, he could almost hear a smile in her words. "You think it's true."

She gave a shrug, suddenly refusing to speak. Then Ms. Engel cleared her throat. "Nathan Jones will be the older gentleman with the hideous black glasses. Calvin Harris will be the overweight one, and Richard Glass will be the one who looks like he just graduated from university."

"Thank you, Ms. Engel."

"Oh, and they're from America, sir," she said when he went to open the door.

He gave a nod and walked inside.

The day went by in a blur. Asher was ushered from one meeting to another, from potential sellers to distributors. Everyone wanted a piece of Dreagan, and with it being the best-selling Scotch on the market for over a hundred years, he understood why.

He walked from his latest meeting, handing a report to Ms. Engel as he did.

"You're five minutes late to your next event, sir."

He saw a bathroom and turned toward it.

"Sir," Ms. Engel began.

Stopping, he faced her. "Unless you want me to take a piss in a jug while I listen to the next group, then you'll give me a minute to take care of business."

"Of course," she hurried to say, clearly embarrassed.

He turned to go into the restroom when something caught his attention out of the corner of his eye. A woman with black hair pulled atop her head had her back to him.

There was something in the way she held her neck that gave him pause. When he saw the thumb ring on her right hand, he immediately thought of Rae.

And that brought a smile to his face.

He couldn't wait until that evening when he hoped to see the enigmatic, beautiful Rae once more. She might wear the latest expensive fashions, but the woman had a serious mind for books.

Asher walked into the restroom and locked the door. Those precious few minutes went by in a blink. The next thing he knew, Ms. Engel hurried him along to the next event on his schedule.

All the while, his thoughts were on Rae. She had been an unexpected surprise. But he hadn't forgotten what Ulrik and the Dark Fae had done to other women a Dragon King happened to show interest in.

A few barely got away with their lives. Though why focus on him when Ulrik had all those at Dreagan to screw around with, he didn't know. But Asher was going to be prepared either way.

It was why he hadn't wholeheartedly agreed to have Rae take him around the city. However, the idea of following other tourists to the sights of the city had its appeal.

When Ms. Engel took him into a large area where the noise was deafening, she hurried to say, "You just have to make an appearance."

His steps slowed when he saw the stage where the double dragon logo of Dreagan filled the entire giant screen behind the table.

A table with one fucking chair.

He was going to kill Con.

"We'll take a few questions," Ms. Engel said as she hurried him to the steps that led to the stage.

As soon as the large, crowded room saw him, they began to clap and shout. He didn't know whether to run away or bask in the glory of such attention. Then he recalled why everyone was so focused on anything to do with Dreagan. Showcased on either side of the table were some of the specialty bottles of whisky Dreagan produced.

He decided not to sit. He took the wireless microphone from the table and lifted it toward his mouth. "Hello."

The crowd erupted, causing him to laugh. He looked over at Ms. Engel to find her smiling. He turned back to the crowd. The lights were dim over the audience, but there was still enough light for him to make out faces.

Once more he caught sight of a woman who reminded him of Rae. It took a moment for him to realize it was the one he'd seen outside the restrooms. She stood off by herself with her phone held up, recording him.

"I hear all of you lads and lasses like Dreagan," he said with a grin.

The cheers grew louder. It seemed to take forever for the crowd to quiet down. Once everyone had taken their seats, he said, "I'm here to take a few questions."

Out of nowhere were people with microphones walking the aisles. Hands shot up in the air. Then a woman's voice with a French accent came over the speakers.

"I love your Scotch. I come every year to the WWC in order to hear what's in store for Dreagan."

"Thank you," he replied. "We appreciate that."

"I'm not the only one who is waiting for you to respond to the video that has gone viral."

Of course this would be his first question. Asher made another mental note to kill Con a second time. He smiled at the woman. "I could pretend I doona know what video you speak of, but that wouldna be fair to all of you."

"So you're going to tell us the truth?" someone shouted from the very back.

Asher was going to have to give them an answer without actually giving them an answer. He didn't want to lie, because he had a feeling it wouldn't be long before the truth was out. So he had to come up with another way.

"We all love the fantastical stories whether they're fantasy or paranormal. We all love the idea that J.R.R. Tolkien's Middle Earth is actually real, even though it isna. If there were dragons, there would be some evidence to prove that fact, aye?"

* * * *

Rachel's gaze was glued to Asher as she held her phone up to record him. He knew how to work a crowd even though he wasn't at all happy about having to be up there. He made the best of the situation and worked the room like a professional. She didn't want to admire him for it, but damn if she couldn't seem to help herself.

Then came the first question. She waited for the lie, but that's not what passed his lips. What the zealous crowd didn't realize was that he answered their question with a question.

She had to give him props for not outright lying, but he hadn't told the truth either. And to use books and movies that had captured the world only seemed to help him sell the non-answer.

"Are you a dragon?" someone yelled.

He looked down at himself. "I look pretty human to me."

The Dragon Kings could be human or dragon, so again he hadn't lied. But omission of a fact was as much as lying.

His gaze landed on her for a second time. She wasn't worried about him noticing her. Not only was she in a pair of jeans and a bulky sweater, but her hair was up, she wore blue colored contacts, and she applied her makeup so that it appeared she didn't have any on—when in fact it changed the shape of her nose, chin, and forehead.

She waited as Asher took a deep breath. He slowly released it and looked around the room. Maybe it was the way he stood or how his shoulders bunched slightly, but she knew he was about to say something big.

"I'm supposed to be up here talking about our whisky, but I can tell none of you are satisfied with my answers. So let me pose one to you," Asher said. "Do you believe in dragons?"

There was a multitude of reactions varying from it was absolute nonsense to someone who swore they'd seen one. Rachel listened, but she kept her eyes on Asher.

He laughed as someone pointed out the dragons on the Dreagan whisky. "Dreagan is Gaelic for dragon. We're Scots who like to acknowledge our ancestors. Of course we use dragons as our symbols."

A man took a microphone from someone. He cleared his throat, then in a deep German accent asked, "Did Dreagan put out the video?"

"I wish we had," Asher replied. "It would've been a great promotion, but I would've done things a bit differently. We obviously didna put out the video because it has drawn attention from media outlets and authorities of every division across all countries."

"Is it affecting your sales?" asked another man.

Asher shook his head. "Dreagan sells itself. It doesna matter who runs the company or who stands up here answering questions. The whisky is the finest there is, and it proves that year after year."

Murmurs of agreement ran through the room.

A woman took the mic next. "What are the authorities looking for?"

"Dragons," he answered.

To her amazement, Asher remained on the stage for another half hour answering some of the same questions again and again. He remained polite and respectful through it all.

No one asked him again if Dreagan was really the home of dragons. His talk seemed to dissuade some who were disappointed he wasn't a dragon.

She wondered what everyone would think if she could somehow make him shift in front of them. Most likely not even that would hurt

Dreagan sales. In fact, it might make the sales double.

When he called an end to the questions, he quickly quieted the upset crowd by offering everyone a taste of two of Dreagan's most expensive Scotches.

That was her cue to duck into the shadows moments before Asher came down the steps to join his assistant. He blew out a breath, laughing as the small woman fell in step with him.

"Good job, sir," she replied.

Rachel counted to twenty before she followed them. All day she'd been on Asher's heels, and he hadn't even known it. She might not have been able to go into every meeting, but she knew where he was, who he met with, and how long he remained.

He hadn't eaten a single bite. She'd stuffed half a sandwich in her mouth to calm her rumbling stomach, but all she'd seen Asher have was a bottle of water.

She snorted when a woman practically threw herself in front of him to get his attention. The woman ended up tripping over her own feet and falling on her face.

Rachel had a hard time not laughing out loud. He quickly went down on one knee and helped the woman to her feet, being a complete gentleman the entire time. He didn't say a word when the woman handed him a piece of paper that most likely had her number on it.

He slid it in the inside pocket of his suit and gave her a smile as he walked off. That woman wasn't the only one after Asher. There were few there that hadn't set their sights on him.

She waited for him to flirt or take one back to the hotel with him, but he didn't.

"You have ten minutes to get to your dinner, sir," his assistant said as she motioned to the doors and the car waiting for him.

Rachel stilled when his gaze ran over her before jerking back to her face. He stared at her a second before walking out.

Perhaps she needed to ensure she looked nothing like Rae. The last thing she wanted was for him to learn Rae was actually Rachel.

Chapter Five

It felt like an eternity before Asher arrived at the hotel. He briefly contemplated going up to his room to change, but he wanted to see Rae too desperately.

He strode into the bar, his gaze sweeping the room. But he didn't see her. The disappointment was swift and engulfing. It was looking forward to talking to Rae that had gotten him through the day. And now she wasn't even there.

"Looking for someone?" a voice asked behind him.

He turned to find Rae. His mouth went dry when he saw the silvery off-the-shoulder sweater skimming her curves before flaring at her waist. Paired with black skinny pants that zipped at the ankle and black stilettos, she was a vision.

The expanse of creamy skin exposed made him long to touch her. He held himself back. Barely.

Her long tresses were down once more. She wore no necklace this time. Her only jewelry was diamond stud earrings, a silver bangle, and her thumb ring.

"Still want that drink?" she asked.

He held out his arm for her. "I want your company more than anything."

"Flattery?"

"Truth."

Her brown eyes sparkled before she turned her head forward. Asher walked her inside and found a table in the back. In moments, they placed a drink order, but when he saw her glance at the food on the table next to them, he waved the waiter back to them and ordered several appetizers.

"How was your day?"

She shrugged and accepted her wine from the waiter. "Uneventful.

Yours?"

"Long."

She smiled at his choice of words. "And busy, I presume?"

"It nearly took an act of God to get my PA to allow me a few seconds to find a restroom."

"What do you do to keep you on such a tight schedule?"

He took a long drink of his whisky while he regarded her. Everyone seemed to know who he was and where he was from. Could Rae be different? How refreshing.

"I'm here for the World Whisky Consortium."

Her eyebrows shot up in her forehead. "Ah. Which explains why you love Scotch."

"Aye." He raised his glass to her and took another drink.

"Do you work for a distillery or a distributor?"

"Distillery."

She leaned forward, placing one elbow on the table. "Do you like it?"

"I love it. I've been involved for as long as I can remember. There is something about taking part of the land and combining it to make something as savory as a good whisky."

"What's the brand? Would I have heard of it?"

He hesitated, wondering if she would change once she knew the truth. "Dreagan."

"Oh," she said with wide eyes. "I do recognize that brand. I'm not a whisky drinker myself."

"You're missing out."

She smiled before bringing the wine to her lips. "Am I?"

"Aye." His balls tightened at the lowering of her voice.

He was finding it harder and harder to keep his hands to himself and not lean forward and take her lips. Did she have any idea how he hungered for a taste of her?

The conversation was interrupted as the food arrived. Asher watched Rae immediately reach for one of the lobster bites. She was discreet and elegant, but there was no denying she was starving. He kept the talk light until she finally sat back with a satisfied smile.

She noticed him watching and wrinkled her nose. "I guess I was hungry."

"Did you no' eat dinner?"

"I had other things going on," she replied and finished her wine.

"You should've told me."

Rae waved away his words. "It's fine. Thank you for ordering the food."

"It's my pleasure."

"Want to get out of here?"

"And go where?" he asked, intrigued.

She smiled and rose to her feet. "Come with me."

He let the bartender know they were done and to put the bill on his room, then he followed Rae into the lobby. A bellman was helping her into a long black coat. She buttoned and belted it before tucking her hands in the pockets with a smile directed at him.

It had been a long time since Asher felt so…exuberant. And it was all because of her. She captivated him in every way possible. She was elegant and enthusiastic, sophisticated and dynamic.

And she pulled it off effortlessly.

With his hand on her back, they walked from the hotel onto the sidewalk. He followed her as she turned and wandered seemingly with no destination in mind.

"Where are we going?" he asked.

She glanced at him with a grin. "Does it matter?"

Actually it didn't. Gone were the sounds of the bar and hotel. Out on the streets it was quieter, softer with the night around them.

"No," he answered.

They walked for a time in the shadows and shine of the streetlights without talking. Asher was really seeing the city as he hadn't while in the car. He listened to traffic as it zoomed by, watched as people walked past them, and smelled the many delicious scents of restaurants, bakeries, and cafés.

They stopped next to the Seine River and stared at the Eiffel Tower aglow with lights. He felt Rae's gaze on him and turned to her.

"You're having a good time."

He was surprised that she was taken aback by that fact. "Aye. And happy about it. Thank you for this."

"I didn't do anything."

"You got me out of the hotel. You allowed me to see, smell, hear, and feel the city as I couldna do any other way."

His words seemed to flummox her as she glanced away. A second later, she had her composure back in place. "Tell me of Dreagan."

"Dreagan," he said, thinking of his home.

* * * *

Rae watched the way his eyes took a faraway look as he murmured the name of his home. The smile he wore bespoke of his love in ways words never could. She thought it would be a safe subject after seeing him enjoy their simple walk that had affected her so. How wrong she was.

But she couldn't look away. Whatever thoughts she had to lead him about on a merry chase of desire and lust took a backseat somehow. She wasn't sure how or when it happened.

If something like this had occurred in the past, she would've ended the night until she could set them back on course. Asher wasn't just unexpected in every way, but he constantly astounded her. It was genuine delight she saw on his face and in his eyes as they walked. She loved the simple pleasures in life, and it appeared as if they had something else in common.

Rachel waited with baited breath. She told herself it was a part of her undercover work.

"Dreagan is Scotland," Asher said. "The land draws you in a way you can no' begin to understand. You feel the majesty and magic of the ancient land. From the tallest mountain to the lowest valley, in the leaves of the trees and in the currents of the streams, you feel an overwhelming and unshakable need to want to be a part of such a place. To want to belong.

"It doesna confine you. Instead, it cradles you, offering its beauty and solitude for those who answer its call. It's wild and free. It's fierce and unbreakable. It's home."

Rachel had the urge to board a plane right that moment and travel to Dreagan so she could see all that he just spoke of. In his words, his soul was laid bare.

In those precious few moments, she saw just how much Dreagan meant to him. It was in his heart and his psyche. It anchored him in a way that spoke to her, answering a plea she hadn't realized she held.

His arm wrapped tighter around her, drawing her into his warmth. She was suddenly cold. It was a bone-deep chill that she feared she might never shake.

Because he'd made her think of the past, of her home where she had been deliriously happy. In a naïve, childish way she'd assumed life would always be so wonderful.

Until it wasn't.

"Lass, talk to me."

She heard the worry in his words, heard the deepening of his voice.

Unable to help herself, she lifted her face in order to see him. "I'm fine."

"You're no'. What is it?"

"You love your home."

There was a beat of silence before he said, "Aye."

"You're lucky."

"Did you no' love your home?"

"I loved it with all my heart." A picture of her parents and sister flashed in her head.

He didn't ask questions or push for an explanation. No, he did something even worse. He simply held her, letting her drift with her memories.

What was wrong with her? What was it about Asher that kept her from her plan? Why did she allow his words and actions to push past her end goal?

She knew what he was from her research about Dreagan and what little Sam had told her regarding those who lived there. She knew Asher wasn't human, but a dragon in the guise of a handsome man.

Sam had showed her how deceitful and devious the Kings were by hiding their true selves and using magic to keep humans from a large portion of the sixty thousand acres that was Dreagan. All the Dragon Kings were cunning, beautiful liars who had conned an entire race into believing they were as human as the rest of them.

Sam also cautioned her that the Dragon Kings easily seduced women, but they could also turn on a dime and kill without hesitation. The seduction she believed, but the killing…? That she wasn't so sure of. Sam hadn't provided any proof of a King killing a mortal, and neither had her research.

Perhaps that's why she hadn't felt any fear with Asher. Though she wasn't sure why she didn't pull away and put some distance between them. Why didn't she feel the same revulsion for Asher as she had two days earlier?

Rachel put her hands on the cold metal of the railing and drew in a shaky breath. Asher's other hand came to rest atop hers. It was a simple gesture, but it rooted them to that spot, that very instant.

Her gaze was on their hands even as he gently turned her to face him. His fingers brushed her chin. Slowly, her eyes rose to his. The hand he had on her back pulled her closer—and she didn't resist. She wasn't sure she could, even if she wanted.

And she didn't want to.

Every nerve ending sizzled, crackled with excitement and…

anticipation. She held her breath, unsure of what she felt or why she was experiencing it.

Then his head lowered and she didn't care. Their breaths billowed from their lips, mixing together before vanishing into the night.

She gazed into his striking green eyes and saw the lights reflected in his depths. But more than that, she saw the hunger, the yearning within. Her stomach quivered at the tangible desire swirling between and around them.

No longer did she feel even a hint of the cold. Every one of her senses was filled with Asher. And she...liked it.

When his lips touched hers, something electric zapped through her, causing her to suck in a sharp breath in surprise. He pulled back enough to look at her. This was the time she should call it a night, walk away and regroup for the next day.

Instead, she lifted her face to his. She had to experience more of him, to feel his kiss and know his taste.

When his mouth claimed hers, his tongue slid along the seam of her lips. They parted for him, on their own accord, granting him access to do as he wished. His arms wrapped around her, holding her securely. With a sigh, she melted against him.

She tasted the whisky on his tongue. The exotic taste mixed with his kiss caused her blood to heat. Her hands splayed on his chest before moving upward to lock around his neck. With a groan that rumbled his chest, he deepened the kiss.

Then something strange happened. Warmth spread through her, settling low in her belly. At first she thought she was going to be sick, but the more he kissed her, the more the warmth grew—until it was a fire.

And did it rage.

It burned brightly, scalding her with its intensity. She couldn't breathe, couldn't think. And she didn't care. All that mattered was that he continue kissing her, taking her further along this incredible journey.

Then that wasn't enough. She wanted...no, she *needed* more. As if sensing her thoughts, he turned her so that her back was to the railing. His heat surrounded her. Every breath she drew into her lungs was filled with his scent of dark amber and mahogany. The longer they kissed, the more fiery and out of control their kisses became.

It was Asher who gradually pulled away. She struggled to find words, to tell him she didn't want it to end. Her lids slid closed when his thumb ran over her bottom lip and he groaned.

She leaned into him, hoping he would kiss her again. This

feeling…this sensation…was awful and amazing. She didn't know whether to fight it or give in, but her body didn't give her a choice.

Asher didn't say a word as he laced his fingers with hers and turned toward the hotel. They walked in silence once more, becoming more in tune to him with every step she took. She could literally feel their souls intertwining and melding.

She should be scared, and she was. But she was also excited and aroused to the point that she wanted to crawl out of her skin. He'd done that to her. When no other had caused even a hint of desire, he had brought an inferno.

When they reached the elevator of the hotel, he pressed the *eight* button for his floor and looked at her. She knew what he was asking. Her mind warned her to leave for the night, but her body begged her to experience more of what he had so easily unleashed.

She stood beside him, facing the door. Out of the corner of her eye she saw him grin. It was a pleased smile, one that said her decision made him happy.

Almost as happy as she was.

Chapter Six

Asher didn't want to think about the passionate kisses he shared with Rae or why he couldn't seem to get enough of her. The more he tasted and touched, the more he craved.

The more he *hungered.*

As they walked into the penthouse suite, all he cared about, all that mattered was the woman beside him. Desire burned deep, swirling through his muscle and bone like tendrils of flames.

It consumed him until he thought he might go mad with the force of such passion. Lust he'd experienced before, but this was so much more. It went beyond the physical.

He thought of all the Kings who'd found mates, and it stopped him dead in his tracks. Why was he thinking about mates? But then he knew—Rae.

Their hands remained joined as he bolted the door and walked her into the suite. Her dark eyes burned brightly, her lips still swollen from his kisses.

His already straining cock jumped as he thought of taking her in his arms again. He wanted to mark her as his, to claim her in such a way that everyone who looked at her would know she was his.

It should scare the hell out of him. But all he felt was a kind of peace. As if his soul had found what it had been looking for. Which couldn't be right. He'd been satisfied on his own.

He halted and faced Rae. She turned to him, her wide lips slightly parted and the pulse at her throat beating wildly. He unbelted her coat and slowly released each button. Then he pushed the thick garment over her shoulders.

It fell to the ground at her feet, forgotten as she put her hands on his chest. She hadn't seemed to notice that he'd gone into the night with nothing more than his suit, and that was fine with him. He didn't want to answer any questions.

Her hands ran down the front of his charcoal gray suit as if feeling the fabric. Then she unbuttoned it. Those dark, seductive eyes of hers lifted, staring at him through her thick, black lashes.

And just as he'd done, she smoothed her hands up to his shoulders, shoving the jacket off. He shifted his arms so the garment slid off with a slight *whoosh*. His hands rested on her waist, feeling the curve of her hip. A moan stirred when she bit her lip and moved closer. The woman had him aching already, and he hadn't even begun to make love to her.

In the millions of years he'd been on the realm, he'd had many women. But not a single one was anything like Rae. He saw the desire in her eyes, but there was hesitancy as well. As if she wasn't sure what to do.

The fact she was so confident in their conversations and flirting— this stunned him. She needed to know she could do whatever she wanted.

He saw the way she gripped his shirt at his throat with both hands. He gave her a smile. "I'm yours, lass. Do what you will."

Her gaze lowered to her hands, and a slow smile pulled at her lips. Then, with a yank, she tore open his shirt.

He had to fist his hands not to grab her as she gazed at his bare chest with blatant pleasure. Her touch was soft as her fingers glided over his chest and stomach. She grew bolder and flattened both hands on him as she caressed over his torso. It wasn't long before he yanked off the shirt so she could touch more of him.

The pleased look on her face made it even harder for him not to undress her as he longed to do. He closed his eyes and enjoyed the feel of her hands on him, learning him.

All of a sudden, her caresses stopped. He opened his eyes to find her gaze locked on his tattoo. It had been a part of him for so long that he sometimes forgot it was there.

Her eyes were fastened on his left arm where the dragon sat perched between his shoulder and elbow with the appearance of its long talons sunk into Asher's skin, with its wings tucked against him. The dragon had a snarl, his head facing Asher.

He wondered how Rae saw the tattoo. Would she question the mix of black and red ink that couldn't be duplicated? Would she wonder why the dragon was on that arm?

Remaining still, he waited as she ran her finger down the tail of the dragon, from his elbow to the point of his wrist and back up again. Then she let those same fingers glide over the dragon's wings and body before stopping at the head, which was at his shoulder.

After a moment, her gaze shifted to his. There was something altogether different in her eyes. He didn't know what it was, but he didn't like it. There was no way he was going to lose what had flared to life so effortlessly between them. He cupped her face with both hands and kissed her.

It wasn't a slow, sedate kiss like earlier. It was carnal and erotic. He shamelessly seized her lips in an attempt to once more reveal the woman who so eagerly tore open his shirt and touched him.

There was a heartbeat of panic when she didn't respond, then with a sigh, her arms wrapped around his neck. She returned his kiss with wanton abandon that made his balls tighten.

He then slowly walked her backward to his bedroom, never breaking the kiss. Rae's passion matched his own. He'd never encountered a woman who could make him ache as she did.

In the bedroom, he broke the kiss long enough to pull her sweater over her head and toss it aside. Beneath it she wore a silvery strapless bra that he found insanely arousing. It was Rae who removed her shoes and unzipped her pants. His mouth went dry. The flaps fell open, revealing her naval and the lacy edge of her panties.

No longer could he hold back. He grasped Rae, yanking her against him and kissing her savagely. Her hands plunged into his hair, nails scraping his scalp as she clutched handfuls of hair.

A frenzy took them as they continued to kiss and remove the remainder of each other's clothes. In a matter of moments, they were skin to skin. He ran his hand down her spine and over her hip. He loved the feel of her silken skin and the way her body reacted to his touch.

He sucked in a breath when her long fingers wrapped around his cock. The kiss ended as he looked down at her. She stroked him as if it was the only thing she wanted to do. A bead of pre-cum formed and she smeared it over the crown of his rod before she brought her thumb to her mouth and wrapped her lips around her finger, sucking.

Something inside him snapped. He had to be inside her, right then or die. His arms lashed around her before lifting her and laying her on the bed. Her long dark tresses fanned around her as she reached for him. He knelt between her open legs and leaned down to kiss her once more.

He reached between them and cupped her breast, feeling the weight of it as her nipple hardened in his palm. With a shift of his body, he groaned before taking the peak into his mouth and teasing it with his tongue.

She moaned loudly, her back arching off the bed as her nails dug into his shoulders. He suckled the nipple harder to hear her cries of pleasure.

When he moved to her other breast, he tweaked the turgid peak with his fingers before wrapping his lips around it. Her cries grew louder by the moment while her hips rocked against him seeking release to the growing passion.

He wanted to spend hours loving her—and he would. But at that moment, they were both too worked up for a lengthy session of lovemaking. He flattened his palm on her stomach and moved his hand downward until he reached her sex.

Her legs fell open and her breath locked in her lungs. He lifted his head to look at her while he lightly ran his fingers over her swollen sex. He helplessly thrust his hips when he found her wet. How he wanted to plunge inside her right that instant, but somehow he held back. He slid a finger inside her, then added a second before thrusting.

Her breath released in a rush. He couldn't take his eyes from her face as surprise and pleasure washed over her in varying degrees. Her hips began moving in time with his fingers, silently urging him on.

He let his thumb swirl over her clit. Her entire body tensed for a second before she cried out, wanting more. He pumped his fingers faster, teasing her clit with every other thrust.

Sweat broke out over his body as he fought to keep control over his need. Asher then moved between her legs and replaced his fingers with his tongue.

"Asher," she moaned.

He held her hips in place as he flicked his tongue over her swollen clit. With her cries filling the room, he teased her until her body began to tighten.

Only then did he rise up. She opened her eyes, their gazes meeting. He guided himself to her entrance. Then he watched her eyes widen as the head of his cock slid inside her. Her hands twisted the covers when he slowly pushed himself forward until half of him was inside her. Then he pulled out and thrust hard, seating himself fully.

She screamed his name and reached for him. He placed his hands on either side of her head as he began to drive into her. Soon, they were clinging to each other as the passion rose high.

He rocked his hips faster, plunged deeper, and when he felt the walls of her tight sex clamp around him a second before she screamed his name, he lost all control and climaxed with her.

As her body milked him, he found himself floating high from the exquisite pleasure.

Minute by minute, they came down from the euphoria but remained locked in each other's arms. For the first time in more years than Asher could remember, he felt as if fortune had finally smiled upon him.

Because in his arms was the best thing that had ever happened to him.

Chapter Seven

Rachel knew it was wrong to stay with Asher, but every time she tried to talk herself into leaving, she couldn't manage it. She was comfortable with his strong arms around her. He made her feel sheltered and secure.

Odd since he was the thing she was supposed to be afraid of.

How had it happened? How had she found herself in his bed? There had been a brief second when she saw his dragon tattoo where she recalled what her goal was. Then she promptly forgot all about it when he kissed her again.

She didn't want to admit it, especially not to herself, but she had a feeling she experienced her first run-in with desire. And it had been glorious.

That could be the only reason. Why else couldn't she keep her hands off him or her clothes on? What other reason was there for her to keep kissing him? Or for her to want him to make love to her? Or to forget about protection?

It wasn't just the desire, it was the absolute pleasure she found in his arms. The man—dragon—must be a master. Then again, if she'd been around since the beginning of time, she'd be a master at sex too.

The suite was quiet as Asher slept. A part of her had actually wondered if the Dragon Kings did sleep, but she had her answer. She turned onto her back and stared at the ceiling.

She was up to her neck in this shit. And that's what it was. Shit.

Not once had she ever used her body for a story. Though, technically, she hadn't actually used her body. It had been freely given because there had been no way she was walking away from such amazing kisses.

He wasn't supposed to be this wonderful. He was gallant and charming and a true gentleman. It was an act. She needed to remember that. It was all just an act so that the Dragon Kings could continue on as they always had.

But what was their end goal? Surely they didn't want to hide forever. That made her stop. Why had they been hiding? If they were as powerful as she'd seen in that video, why hadn't they taken over the world? Why were they doing everything in their power to turn attention away from that leaked video?

And why hadn't she asked herself this before?

She admonished herself. She was a better journalist than this. Was she so blinded by what Sam told her and making a name for herself by going after a company as big as Dreagan that she had forgotten basic rules of her trade?

Like investigating everything and everyone.

It was the first time she'd made such a mistake, and she wasn't proud of it. Sam had been so convincing, as had that video. The research on Dreagan had been damning as well, with the lack of documents, signatures, names, and even photos of those running Dreagan Industries. In her eyes, there hadn't been a need to dig deeper.

But there was always a need—because there was always another side to the story.

She turned her head on the pillow and looked at Asher, who lay on his side facing her. The window behind him had the curtains open but the sheers pulled closed. Moonlight poured into the room, spilling onto the bed and his magnificent body.

She recalled how it felt to run her hands over every wonderfully hard muscle of his body from his shoulders to his chiseled abs to his long legs and amazing butt. A man shouldn't have such a fine ass, but that was just one of his assets. She licked her lips and rolled toward him once more.

Unable to help herself, she placed her palm on his shoulder and slowly ran it down his arm to his hand that lay between them. He had long, thick fingers. His nails were trimmed neatly without even a single hangnail. She stroked down each of his fingers, remembering how those hands had awoken the desire inside her.

Why did it have to be Asher? Why couldn't it have been someone else? What did he have that others didn't?

She smiled ruefully because the answer was very clear—he was a dragon, but not just any dragon. He was an *immortal* Dragon King.

Sam told her of their immortality, but it had been something she'd witnessed in Asher's eyes that confirmed that fact for her. *Endlessness.*

Of all the men all over the world, it had to be Asher. Just thinking of how he'd roused her carnal side, her blood heated. Her gaze ran down his body to see his arousal thick and hard.

Her gaze jerked to his face to find those stunning green eyes open and watching her. She physically ached for his touch, to have his lips on hers once more.

To feel him deep inside her.

He was the enemy. Wasn't he? It scared the hell out of her that it didn't matter who he was. She knew the truth of Asher, knew he was a man second only to being a dragon. It should jar her out of her desire-soaked mind and remind her what she set out to do. Instead, she was drowning in his eyes.

"I hope you were no' thinking of leaving."

She swallowed. "No."

"Good. I'm no' nearly finished with you yet."

Her heart skipped a beat when he pulled her close. His large hand rested on her hip before sliding over and down her ass cheek to her leg. A knowing grin pulled at his lips when his hand stopped behind her knee. Then he tugged her leg up so that it rested on his hip.

The air hit her sex and chills raced over her skin. Asher had yet to do anything and already the anticipation was too much to handle. She was a ball of nerves, anxious and hungry for more of what he so willingly gave.

"What do you want, *a ghràidh*?"

His brogue was enough to make her swoon, but when he spoke the other language, she melted. She thought it might be Gaelic, but she didn't ask. Just as she didn't ask what it meant. How could she when his hand was moving slowly up and down her leg so that his fingers were coming so close to touching her sex?

A shuddering breath passed her parted lips when a thick digit sank inside her. With just a look, he restrained her, locking her gaze with his.

Slowly, his finger began to pump in and out of her. He had complete control over her body, her soul, and even her thoughts. He deftly and deliberately stroked her body to a fever pitch with one finger.

Each time she moved her hips, his finger stilled. It was maddening, this driving need to move and add friction, only to have him stop. His smile said he knew exactly what he did to her. And, God help her, she craved more. His touch was becoming like oxygen. She needed it in order to live.

"The first time was too quick," he murmured as he nipped at her lips. "I'm going to brand myself on you so that whenever you dress, wash, or even think of being with someone else, all you'll feel, see, and want is me."

Dear God. She was in deeper than she realized because she knew without a doubt he could do exactly as his words promised.

"What do you think of that?"

She had a hard time remembering his question as a second finger joined the first and moved deep within her. "I…I want that."

What? Did those words just come out of her mouth? But it was the truth. No amount of excuses could change that. She couldn't even blame him, because he hadn't seduced her. The blame for that lay squarely on her shoulders.

"Doona move," he warned as his fingers increased their tempo.

He had to be joking. It went against every fiber of her being to remain still as he stroked her so thoroughly. She was so focused on what his hand was doing that she jerked when his lips wrapped around a nipple.

He sucked hard, the pull on the peak like a direct line to her sex. Then his tongue swirled around her nipple before he lightly nipped it and sucked again. She clung to him, her body shaking as she fought not to move lest he stop the pleasurable torment.

His fingers pushed deep and remained there as the heel of his hand pressed against her clit while he suckled harder. To her absolute shock, an orgasm ripped through her. The intensity of it took her breath. A cry lodged in her throat as she had no choice but to ride the delicious waves of pleasure.

He prolonged the climax by moving his fingers inside her. She had no idea how long it lasted, but when she finally came down and was able to open her eyes, he leaned over her.

If it was possible, she hungered for him even more. It wasn't solely because he knew how to work her body, but because he understood what she needed.

And he gave it to her.

She hadn't even known what she needed until him. Now that he was in her arms, she wasn't sure she could ever let go. Or ever want to.

He leaned down until their mouths brushed. She rose up to capture his lips, but he rubbed the length of his cock along her sensitized sex. Instantly, her hips lifted. She tried to grab his arms, but before she knew it, he turned her onto her side and molded his body to hers from the back.

His arousal pressed into her back hard and hot. He held her breasts in his hands, massaging them. She squeezed her legs together as a rush of desire ran through her. She moaned when his fingers squeezed her nipples. His mouth was at her neck, kissing and licking while his warm breath fanned over her.

"Lift your leg," he bade.

Without hesitation, she did as he asked. He shifted, and she felt his cock against her as his leg came between hers. She arched her back when he pinched her nipples.

"Please," she begged. "I need you inside me."

"And I need inside you," he whispered huskily. He murmured something she couldn't understand. Then he said, "Take me, Rae. Bring me inside you."

She grew hot just thinking about it. She reached down and took his length in hand. She loved the feel of him and couldn't help running her hand up and down him a few times.

He groaned, his hips moving in time with her. The idea that he could possibly crave her as much as she did him made her bold. She cupped his ball sack and rolled them in her hands.

He hissed before he ground out her name with a mixture of hunger and wonder that made her smile. Unable to hold off a moment longer, she brought the blunt head of his cock to her opening.

She felt her own wetness. In all her life, she'd never been so turned on by anyone. Now she understood why people did crazy things when desire ruled them. Because that same rush, that same compelling need controlled her.

All thoughts fled as he slid inside her. She sighed as he filled her, stretching her. It felt so right to have him inside her. As if that was where he belonged.

As if that was what she'd been anticipating without ever knowing it.

Her eyes closed on a moan when he began to move. She put her hand on his hip and felt his muscles bunch and shift beneath her palm. That powerful body of his was wrecking havoc upon hers, but it was the most glorious thing she ever experienced.

His hand left her breast and skated down her stomach before his fingers parted her trimmed curls and spread her lips. He paused, teasing her.

"Asher," she begged.

His lips brushed her ear before he nipped the lobe. "I have a fever. It's for you, *a ghràidh*."

"You make me burn."

"Then we'll burn together."

His finger began to swirl over her clit slowly and gained speed gradually, matching his thrusts. All the while, his other hand pinched her nipple before rolling it between his thumb and forefinger.

The onslaught on her body was mind-blowing. She wanted to stay just as they were forever, without the outside world ever intruding on whatever magical hold was upon them.

Desire built rapidly. She loved the feel of his balls slapping against the back of her leg as his hips pumped faster, driving deeper. Their sweat-slicked bodies glided against the other, their breathing harsh and loud. The orgasm was building, leaving her on the precipice of ecstasy.

He gave a slight tug on her clit, and her world shattered again. She was engulfed with pleasure so thick it swallowed her.

"Aye, *a ghràidh*. I can feel you clamping around me. You feel so damn good," he said huskily.

Another wave of bliss slammed into her.

His hand clamped onto her hip as he pulled her back and slammed into her again and again, his hips pumping furiously. He drove into her deep as he called her name. She could feel his cock pulse as he emptied himself inside her, and all she could think was "when can I have him again?"

With her heart thumping wildly, she smiled as he pulled her back against his chest. They lay in silence as their bodies cooled.

"I doona know what brought you into the hotel bar last night, but I'm verra glad you were there."

She snuggled back against him. "So am I. I don't want this night to ever end."

"It doesna have to."

But it did. Her eyes opened as reality crashed upon her.

She couldn't give herself up to him. She had a job to do, and no amount of amazing sex could interfere. Whatever she might've felt a few minutes ago would have to be pushed aside.

She had to remember that with him, she was Rae. And Rae would soon disappear after she had all the information she needed.

Chapter Eight

The morning came much too soon for Asher. Like Rae, he didn't want their night together to end. As powerful as he was as an immortal, he couldn't stop time.

He was just reaching for her when there was a knock on his door. He jumped up, glancing at the clock to see it was the time he'd told Ms. Engel to meet him for breakfast. He grabbed the robe and hurried to belt it on as he walked to the door. When he opened it, there was Ms. Engel with a hotel employee behind her with a cart full of food.

"Did I wake you, sir?" she asked.

"Nay." He moved aside so they could enter.

While Ms. Engel watched over the employee laying out the food on the breakfast table, Asher returned to his bedroom. The door was half-closed. He peeked around it and saw Rae already dressed and putting on her shoes.

"I forgot I had a breakfast meeting," he told her.

She looked up and smiled. "I hadn't intended to stay the night."

"I'm glad you did."

Her deep brown eyes watched him for a moment before she ran a hand through her black hair and stood. "I'm sure you have a busy day ahead. I should leave."

"Stay. Ms. Engel orders enough food for an army. There will be plenty."

"Perhaps another time."

He wasn't ready to let her go—in any fashion. The thought of not being with her the rest of the day didn't sit well. He wanted to look over and see her smile, to hear her opinion on all matters, and to just know that she was near.

He walked her from the bedroom to the door, ignoring the look Ms.

Engel shot them. He almost asked Rae to join him for the day, then he thought about all the boring meetings he had to attend and didn't want to put her through that.

"How about dinner tonight?" He opened the door, standing with his back against it.

Ms. Engel quickly said, "You have a prior engagement."

"Cancel it," he told her while throwing her a quick look.

Rae put a hand on his chest and smiled. "Keep your schedule. We'll meet in the bar again."

"Make sure and eat today."

"Yes, sir," she said with a laugh.

Asher pulled her close for a kiss before reluctantly letting her walk away. She looked over her shoulder, shooting him a smile and a wave before turning the corner.

He grudgingly stepped back and let the door close. Then he faced his assistant. "The dinner can be canceled."

"It won't fit anywhere else in your schedule," she said while pouring coffee into two mugs.

The hotel employee quickly left, leaving them alone. Asher could tell something was wrong. He walked into the dining area and put two heaping spoonfuls of sugar into his coffee. He glanced at Blossom, who wore a black pantsuit just as concealing as her others. "What's bothering you?"

Ms. Engel was quiet so long he began to wonder if she would reply. Then she sighed and held her coffee mug between her hands as she looked out the window. "It's not uncommon for whoever is here from Dreagan to find...comfort...with the fairer sex."

"But?" he prompted when she grew quiet.

"There's something about her."

Intrigued, he pulled out a chair and sat, motioning for her to do the same. "What do you mean?"

"I don't know." She uncovered his omelet and pushed it toward him. "I can't explain it."

"Try."

She finally took her seat, shifting her glasses on her nose. After a sip of coffee, she set it aside and began to butter the toast. Every slice there was.

He ate, watching her. Ever since his arrival, Ms. Engel had been concise in all matters. She knew the answers before he ever asked the questions. So to see her flustered let him know this wasn't something he should ignore.

"She's not been after Mr. Con while he was here the years before," Ms. Engel said. "Which is good. I just have a feeling that I've seen her before."

He nodded, because he'd thought the same thing yesterday about that woman at the WWC. He'd thought it was Rae at first. "We see a lot of people daily. It's easy to mistake someone."

Her eyes jerked to him. "I don't forget a face. There's something wrong here, sir. I wouldn't want to jeopardize whatever is between the two of you, but I felt you should know."

"I see." He swallowed his bite of omelet. "Do you believe she wants to harm me?"

"Dreagan has always been famous. Which tends to draw out the crazies."

He fought not to laugh, because she was serious. But her word choice was humorous.

"Now it's notorious as well," she continued. "I've been with Mr. Con long enough to know he can handle any matter that might arise, and I believe you're cut from that same cloth. So while I don't believe she would try to steal from you, there are other ways to get at a man."

"If you're thinking a child, you need no' worry," he informed her. It wasn't something he'd discussed with Rae, though he'd meant to.

It was a rare thing indeed for a mortal to get pregnant with a King's child. And even if it happened, none of the babies survived. Most died early on in the pregnancy, but the few that lasted to term were stillborn.

Ms. Engel bowed her head briefly. "I didn't mean to pry."

"You didna. You had a valid concern, and I'm relieving you of it. What else could she be after?"

"Anything to do with you or Dreagan. Everyone wants to know the truth."

There was something in the way she said it that made him sit up straighter. Could Blossom Engel know their secret? There's no way Con would've allowed her to see anything, but that didn't mean a smart doer like her couldn't have figured it out herself.

"She'll no' get anything."

Ms. Engel nodded woodenly and buttered a piece of toast for the second time.

He didn't like seeing her so disconcerted. Though he wasn't at all thrilled with the idea of her digging for anything on Rae, if it would give her some peace of mind, he would do it.

"If it will make you feel better, look into Rae," he said before taking another bite of the omelet.

"Really?" she asked excitedly.

He nodded. "I doona want Rae knowing, so be discreet."

"Always. What's her surname?"

Asher hesitated. "I doona know. She's staying in the hotel though."

Until then he didn't realize how little he knew of Rae. It wasn't like him not to learn specifics about a person, but she had enthralled him so deeply he hadn't thought of anything other than claiming her body. Perhaps when the WWC was over, he might stay a few extra days in Paris and get to know her better.

"I'll find her," Ms. Engel said with a firm nod. With that decided, she was once more back in control. She speared a strawberry and flipped open her planner. "You handled yesterday brilliantly. Today is going to be rough though."

Just what he didn't want to hear. He listened as she ran down his itinerary, and again there wasn't five minutes scheduled for a break. With only a few more days of this, he was determined to get through it.

After breakfast and the reworking of a few scheduling conflicts for the next day, he showered and readied for the day. He chose a black pinstripe suit and white shirt.

As he and Ms. Engel rode the elevator down and walked through the lobby to his waiting car, he looked for Rae, but she was nowhere to be found. On the drive to the exhibition centre, he looked at the city with new eyes. Rae had done that to him.

He smiled as he thought of how she'd screamed in pleasure multiple times last night. If he had anything to do about it, she would be screaming again that night.

All too soon they arrived at the centre. He exited the car and nodded a greeting to the photographers, journalists hoping to get some information, and the whisky fans as he walked up the steps to the doors.

Inside, Ms. Engel directed him down a hallway and into the first meeting of the day. On his way inside the room, he spotted the woman from the day before. She had her back to him and a big, floppy black hat atop her head, but he recognized her by the way she held herself and the thumb ring.

It reminded him of Rae.

Apparently he was so into the mortal that everything reminded him of her. It should bother him, but oddly, it didn't. He smiled then and entered the room.

Each time he finished with a meeting, he walked out to find Ms. Engel. He supposed she was going to wait to do any digging on Rae, and that pleased him. Perhaps Ms. Engel would see there was no cause for concern.

She didn't bring it up as the hours passed and they went from one event to another. He had a tasting he had to attend where Dreagan showcased their newest batches, as well as their tried and true versions.

He then went to an exhibit where each of the distilleries and their best Scotch was put on display for attendees to sample. As was his duty, Asher made sure to taste those that were Dreagan's closest competitors.

Along with the display, attendees were asked to rank the whisky for a readers' favorite contest. That wasn't the only contest. The professional whisky judges would also be casting votes for who was the best.

Dreagan had won every year for decades. Everyone wanted to know their secret. Asher couldn't exactly tell them the Dragon Kings had been distilling whisky for thousands of years. Not even the history of the first batch of whisky listed Dreagan.

Con had made sure of that. If it had, there would've been too much attention placed on Dreagan. It was easier and more beneficial to let a mortal have that glory.

While he nodded and spoke to the World Whisky Consortium attendees as they came to the Dreagan booth with the double dragon logo on everything, his mind kept drifting to Rae.

Ms. Engel brought up a good point. He didn't know her last name, and with all the shite the Kings had been through, he should know better than to so blindly trust. Ulrik wasn't just working with the Dark Fae, he also brought in humans. Though Asher didn't believe Rae would have a connection to Ulrik. If she did, Rae would be at the WWC to gain more time with him.

But what did she do during the day? She said she was there on business, but neither of the two times they were together had they discussed her. Always her questions were about him.

She asked about Dreagan, but even now he thought it was because she was curious about it. If she really wanted information, she could've asked more pointed questions. Which, he reminded himself, she hadn't.

So while he didn't think Rae was a threat, he needed to know more about her. Because he didn't like the thread of doubt his lack of knowledge about her caused. Ms. Engel seemed capable enough, but she was busy with his affairs currently.

That left the one true mastermind who could find out all there was to know about Rae—Ryder. He ran all the computers at Dreagan, designing cameras so tiny you never knew they were even there. He monitored Dreagan from his computer room on the third floor of the manor.

And now Ryder wasn't alone. He had Kinsey as his mate, who happened to be another computer expert. Between the two of them, there wasn't anything that couldn't get done.

Asher opened the telepathic link all Dragon Kings had and said Ryder's name in his mind.

A few seconds later Ryder replied, *"Aye."*

"I need a favor."

"I'm here to do thy bidding," Ryder teased.

He watched Dreagan employees hand out taste after taste in their booth. *"There is a guest at my hotel I need information on."*

"I am the King of Information. Name?"

"I only know her first name. Rae."

There was a pause. *"Her?"*

"Doona read anything into this."

"Look around Dreagan, Ash. It's a wee bit hard no' too."

"I'm no' returning from Paris with a mate. I had a nice night with the lass, but I want to be sure she isna connected to Ulrik."

"Good point. The fact you want to know more says she means something. Just noting that fact."

Asher wasn't going to discuss this with Ryder, especially when he wasn't sure of anything himself. He liked Rae. A lot. And he wanted to spend more time with her. Right now, that's all it was.

"Ryder," he warned.

"Fine. All you have is Rae. R-A-E?"

"Aye."

"There's no one listed at the hotel with that name."

Asher frowned before he recalled Rae saying it was a nickname. *"It's short for something, I believe. She mentioned it being a nickname."*

"Just for future use, get the real name."

"Remind me to kick your arse when I get back."

"Are we no' having a good time?" Ryder teased. *"You should see all the photos of you going up on the Internet. You're being labeled a 'Hot Bachelor.'"*

He drew in a breath for patience. *"I doona know how Con does it. Everyone wants a piece of me."*

"You're doing a great job."

He grunted in response.

"Ash, there are two guests who could be your Rae. One is a Raelene Bradford.

The other is Rachel Marek. I'm looking at each as we speak."

He waited for Ryder to find something. Either could be Rae. That is if Rae was the start of her name. It could be a deviation from the end of her name. Or it could have nothing to do with her name at all.

"Both women are in their thirties and checked in alone," Ryder said. *"Want me to keep digging?"*

"Aye. I have to go, but see if either is connected to Ulrik or one of the aliases he uses."

"Consider it done."

Asher severed the link and turned to the outstretched hand of one of Dreagan's favorite distributors. As they spoke, he caught sight of a hand taking a sample of Dreagan whisky and he spotted a thumb ring.

His thoughts immediately went to Rae.

Chapter Nine

Rachel hated whisky. Or she used to. However, it seemed she was rapidly developing a taste for Dreagan.

That could be because she'd also acquired a taste for Asher.

She inwardly groaned. What the hell was wrong with her? Instead of working to find hidden meanings in his words or discovering a lie in them, all she did was listen to that amazing voice and recall how he'd made love to her.

It was an entire wasted day. By the time she walked from the exhibit centre, she felt emotionally drained. Asher was getting into the sleek Jaguar that would take him to his dinner.

She waved down a taxi and chanced another look in his direction. He never got brusque with anyone, no matter how many times they asked him for a picture. His photo was splashed worldwide in magazines, newspapers, and other news media. Then there were the fans.

Fans of Dreagan. Fans of Asher. They swarmed like gnats—men and women alike—getting his picture like he was Luke Evans or Jason Statham.

Those fans put up his pictures on Twitter, Facebook, blogs, Tumblr, and Pinterest as if the world were ending tomorrow. The women practically swooned when he bestowed a smile upon them, and they giggled like schoolgirls when he spoke with that deep Scots brogue. Though, he didn't flirt with a single one of the women.

Much to her delight.

The men stood straighter when Asher was around, watching him as if they could somehow pick up on what made him such a... *man*.

What she wanted to tell them was that the thing that made him so special was singular to him alone. Anyone could put on a handmade suit and be driven around in expensive cars. But the swoon-worthy face, the heart-stopping grin, and those breathtaking eyes were his alone. Just like his compassion and patience.

And she was doing it again. Sam's warning of how the Kings seduced echoed in her mind. Asher and the rest of the Dragon Kings weren't good beings. They were liars and monsters whose secret needed to be told so they couldn't hide anymore.

Except, when she saw Asher amid the humans, she didn't see a beast. She saw a man who was taking time to give those who wanted a picture with him or answer questions. He could walk away like many of the other representatives did. But not Asher. He stayed until the last of the fans were finished with him.

Suddenly, the hairs on the back of her neck stood on end. She looked around for whoever was watching her. Her gaze locked on Ms. Engel, who stood on the second floor of the building looking down at her.

Someone slammed into Rachel, making her lose her balance. When she looked back up at the window, Ms. Engel was gone. But that feeling of being observed lingered. No matter where she looked, she couldn't find who was watching her. But it left her feeling...exposed.

She hurried to the taxi and got inside just as Asher finished taking the last picture. "Follow that Jaguar," she told the driver.

When they arrived at the swanky restaurant, she directed the taxi to drive ahead a little ways before he pulled over. Then she scooted to the edge of her seat and held up a wad of euros.

He went to reach for it, but she jerked it back. "This is for you if you wait here for ten minutes."

The Frenchman smiled. "*Oui, mademoiselle.*"

Rachel tucked the money in the pocket of her purse, slung across her body, and exited the taxi. She walked with purpose down the busy sidewalk even as she watched Asher's large frame unfold from the car and button his suit jacket.

He wasn't wearing a coat despite the frigid temperatures. Only then did she recall he hadn't worn one the previous night either. Apparently, Dragon Kings weren't affected by the cold.

"Lucky them," she murmured and stuck her hands in her coat pockets.

She then pulled off her floppy hat and folded it to tuck in her large purse before she replaced it with a cream and gold beanie to cover her ears against the cold.

Her steps slowed when she neared the restaurant. She peeked inside the windows and saw Asher being escorted to the back of the restaurant and behind closed doors. The doors opened long enough for her to see several of the other whisky distillers at the table. More business. She turned and retraced her steps to the taxi.

It was time for her to return to the hotel and get ready for the night. As well as order some room service since she was starving. It also appeared as if a Dragon King didn't need to eat since it was the second day that he'd gone without lunch and didn't seem affected at all.

Not so her. Her stomach growled and a headache was setting in. She paid the taxi the promised money when he let her off in front of the hotel. As soon as she was in her room, she picked up the phone to call room service.

As she waited for the line to connect, she looked around her suite. Someone had been in there. Somebody besides the maid. Nothing was out of place, but she could still tell that someone had walked through her room and touched her things.

She placed her order while she walked around the suite. She ended in her bedroom and disconnected the call. The food would arrive in thirty minutes. Plenty of time to get a shower and dry her hair.

She set down the phone by her laptop and opened the computer. It was still turned off. And it was password protected. Even if someone had been inside, they wouldn't have gotten anything off her computer.

Which was a good thing since all her searches revolved around Dreagan and Asher. She looked around the suite again. Who would've been in here? The only person that came to mind was Sam MacDonald. Yet Sam was away doing his own information gathering at Dreagan. He never told her who his target was, but his determination to reveal the Dragon Kings to the world exceeded her own.

It was why she'd decided to work with him. Besides all the information he brought her, Sam would stop at nothing to release the truth. Yet it was her name attached to the article that would give value to the facts.

Rachel tapped her finger on the laptop before she went back to check that the door was bolted. She tested the sliding glass door that went out onto the balcony to ensure it was locked. She didn't want another surprise visit from Sam since she still hadn't figured out how he got into her bolted hotel room the last time.

Satisfied that everything was locked up tight, she decided to get in the shower. She stood beneath the hot water longer than she intended, but it felt so good. Her body was sore from her night with Asher, but it made her smile. Never had she been so thoroughly loved.

By the time she got out, there was a knock at the door. She glanced at the clock and quickly pulled on her robe as she made her way to the door. She looked through the peephole to see a hotel employee holding a tray of food. Within minutes the food was left and she was once more alone— with the door bolted.

She curled up in the chair and began to devour the steak and butternut squash. Then she moved on to dessert of chocolate mousse cake that went great with her red wine. With her belly full, she rose and dried her hair as she contemplated the night's attire. Her gaze landed on a dress she'd brought on the off chance she might need it.

She didn't need it, but she wanted to wear it.

For Asher.

* * * *

Asher strode into the penthouse suite and came to a sudden stop when he found Ms. Engel standing in the middle of the living room with pinched lips and her body stiff with rage. He released the door, letting it close behind him. He attempted to see her eyes, but those damn glasses continued to prevent it.

He'd hoped Ms. Engel's initial reaction about Rae had been wrong. He released a sigh. "How long have you been waiting?"

"A few hours," came her cool reply.

He put his hands in his pants pockets and glanced down at the file she clasped before her. "Tell me you have no' been standing the entire time."

"No, sir."

"What has soured you, Ms. Engel?" He glanced at the file again. Ryder had tried to talk to him twice, but Asher hadn't been able to answer him during the dinner.

On the way to the hotel, he'd called to Ryder but hadn't been able to reach him. That and the way Ms. Engel looked left him feeling uncertain about what was discovered.

"My advice, sir, is to never see Rae again."

Asher lifted his brows. It must be that bad. At least by Ms. Engel's standards. And that woman had very high standards.

"Or should I say Rachel," Ms. Engel said tightly.

So that was her real name. What was it Ryder said? Rachel Marek? Aye. That was the name. "She told me Rae was a nickname."

"Did she also tell you what she does?" Ms. Engel asked, her chin lifting in anger.

He shook his head as disappointment rapidly filled him.

"She's a journalist."

The statement hung in the air. He didn't want to believe it, but Ms. Engel had no reason to lie. Con trusted her explicitly, which meant Blossom had been thoroughly vetted by Ryder.

Her expression softened, as if she just realized how harsh her words had been. "I know you liked her."

"She's no' asked for anything."

"She's been at the WWC."

Then Asher knew. It broadsided him like a slap from a dragon's tail. The woman with the thumb ring he kept seeing was Rae, or Rachel. No wonder he kept thinking he saw Rae everywhere. Because he had.

She lied to him, and he wanted to know why. A woman like Rae—Rachel—would never admit to anything if confronted. He would have to play it carefully.

"This stays between us, for now," he told Ms. Engel. "You've done good work. Thank you."

"That's it?" she asked in disbelief.

He gave her a smile because she was acting like a mother hen. And somehow that endeared her to him even more. "No' in the least. I'm going to get to the bottom of things with Rae."

"Rachel," Ms. Engel corrected.

"She'll remain Rae for the moment until she admits everything. Doona fear, now that I know the truth, I'll be guarding each word that falls from my lips."

"You might want to think of guarding your body as well."

He laughed when Ms. Engel looked him up and down with a brow raised knowingly. "I'll be sure to."

"This is for you," she said and set down the file on the coffee table. "My room is here as well. If you need me, you know how to reach me."

He had been given Ms. Engel's mobile number, but she was always there so he hadn't had a reason to contact her. "Thank you."

She walked to the door and paused after she opened it. She turned her dark head to look at him. "I am sorry, sir."

"I am, too, lass."

A sigh escaped him when he was alone. He looked at the file, but he didn't reach for it. Perhaps it was better if he didn't know the particulars.

It didn't sit well that Rae deceived him. He thought they'd had a connection, one that went beyond the physical and mental to become soulful. He didn't need to wonder how she came to be in Paris the same time as him. It all would point back to Ulrik one way or another. It always did.

Unless…this had nothing to do with Ulrik and everything with her wanting to do a story on Dreagan. It was that small thread of hope that he clung to, even though he knew it might blow up in his face.

He walked to the sideboard and opened the bottle of Dreagan. He filled the glass more than half full and took it out on to the balcony. It was chilly with a chance of snow overnight. He didn't feel the biting wind or see the city. His gaze was pointed inward as he went over everything he and Rae had spoken about.

Asher considered himself good at spotting those who might attempt to betray him. He hadn't felt that with Rae. Was he such a sucker for a beautiful woman that he ignored such feelings? No. That wasn't it.

There was more. And he was going to find out what it was.

Chapter Ten

Rachel looked at herself in the full-length mirror and nodded in approval. The form-fitting red dress was just the right amount of sensual and classy. It hit right at her knee, and the three-quarter length sleeves had black lace at the elbow. The boat-neck collar dipped low enough to show a hint of cleavage. The back of the dress pointed to a V halfway down before a row of black buttons stopped at the base of her spine.

Her favorite black Christian Louboutin's with their famous red soles were the perfect additions. Choosing minimal jewelry with the diamond studs and her thumb ring, she grabbed the black clutch and headed downstairs to meet Asher.

On the elevator ride, she found she was nervous and impatient to see him again. It had been so difficult to watch him all day and not go up to him for a kiss. Now, she didn't have to pretend not to know him or hide who she was. This was the time she could show him...what? What did she think she could show him? That she cared?

She closed her eyes and wanted to kick herself. She couldn't care for Asher. He was her target. Nothing was going to stop her from writing her article once she garnered enough information. And after it released, he wouldn't want to have anything to do with her.

But she could pretend. She was good at that. Except, for the first time in her life, she was pretending for herself and not her target.

The doors of the elevator opened and she walked out, her gaze immediately going to the bar. Her steps were light and quick as she made her way to the doorway of the bar. There was a smile in place as she expected to see him at any second.

As she walked into the bar, her eyes scanned each table and man for Asher's face. But he was nowhere to be seen. She didn't let that dampen her mood. She continued to the bar and perched upon one of the stools before ordering a glass of red wine.

As each minute ticked by, she began to fear that he wouldn't come. Then she would admonish herself, because there was no reason for him not to. He didn't know the truth about her or what her goal was. He only thought she was a woman who spent the night in his arms having amazing sex.

It was the first time she found herself sickened by what she was doing. Yes, she exposed truths, but what she was doing to herself and her targets was wrong.

"I hope that frown isna for me," came a deep timbre behind her.

She turned with a smile, genuinely happy to see Asher. "Hi."

"Hi," he said and put his mouth on hers.

He lingered there, letting his tongue brush against her lips before he pulled back. "I've waited all day to see your beautiful face."

"Another busy day?" Why did she feel as if she were floating upon pure happiness when he was near?

He shrugged and motioned to the bartender for his drink. "I'm just glad the business part of it is over, and I can have time with you."

"I like the sound of that." She told herself to ask him something about Dreagan, but the words wouldn't make it past her lips.

"Let's take our drinks up to my suite."

More alone time? She was more than okay with that. "I guess that means you don't want to take another walk through the streets," she teased.

He leaned down until his mouth was next to her ear. "I doona want to waste another second sharing you with the world. And as good as that dress looks on you, I want you out of it."

She actually shivered at his words, they affected her so. "Let's go," she said and slid off the stool.

Wine in hand, she walked to the lobby with Asher at her side. He smiled down at her in the elevator, but other than his hand on her back, he didn't touch her.

Inside his suite, she marveled at the view of the city. She hadn't remembered seeing it the night before. Then again, her attention had solely been on Asher. She turned to him as he took her hand and brought her to the sofa. There he removed his jacket and half-faced her as he sat.

"I like you, Rae."

Her heart skipped a beat, because she hadn't realized how much she wanted to hear those words until they'd been spoken. "I like you, too."

"There are many women who attempt to gain my attention because of my affiliation to Dreagan."

She sipped her wine, wondering where he was going with this.

"You doona seem to care what it is I do."

Oh, God. Now she had to lie. And she didn't want to. Then she realized there was a truth she could tell. "I don't care what it is you do. I want to know you."

"And I want to know you. Whatever this is between us is strong. Do you feel it?"

Did she ever. "Yes."

"I doona know where this might lead, but I'd like to find out."

"Yes." The response was out of her mouth with no way to take it back. Her stomach fell to her feet. Why oh why hadn't she stopped herself from answering?

But she knew the answer. She wanted to explore whatever this was with Asher. If only he wasn't a job.

"You know more of me than I know of you," he said. "Tell me about yourself."

She looked down at her hands and spotted the thumb ring. It was a piece of jewelry she never took off, no matter what. That part of her life she didn't speak of with anyone, and yet she found herself turning to Asher and saying, "My family is dead."

"I'm so sorry," he said, his face lined in a frown as he rested his arm on the back of the sofa.

"I've been on my own since I was seventeen."

"What happened?"

She took a drink of wine, gathering the courage to say the awful words last spoken in her therapist's office. "My parents were the typical strict parents. They wanted to know who we were with, their phone numbers, address, and names of their parents. We lived in a relatively small town, so my parents knew nearly all of the parents to mine and my sister's friends."

"Did you have a curfew?"

"Oh, yes. We weren't allowed to date until we were sixteen. My sister was two years older than me, and it was torture watching her go out while I had to wait."

Asher took a drink of his whisky. "I had an older sister and two younger brothers. I remember how that felt."

She never imagined Asher having family. Now that he'd shared such information, he was moving further and further from being just a job. Making it even more difficult for her to do the task she'd come for.

She sipped her wine. "My sister, Rebecca, had a lot of admirers. She always followed the rules and never did anything that might go against what our parents wanted.

"When she brought Ted home, we thought he was perfect for her. He was a freshman in college, came from a large family, and knew what he wanted for his future."

Asher's brows drew together. "So what was the problem?"

"Nothing. At first." She felt that same anxiety that once plagued her threaten to return. She drank deeply, letting the pinot noir settle in her stomach. "My once vibrant, outgoing sister began to retreat into herself. She stopped going to church, stopped being a part of conversations, and began failing subjects in school that she'd always maintained top grades."

Rachel leaned forward and set aside her glass. After all these years it was still difficult for her to talk about it. Rebecca had been her best friend. They shared everything, but Rebecca hadn't opened up to her.

She blew out a breath. "Nothing we said or did seemed to help. The more we tried, the more my sister would lash out at us. She wouldn't eat and was losing weight rapidly. One night, I walked in on her undressing to take a shower. I saw the cigarette burns and bruises all over her. But it was the emotional abuse that had taken the most out of her.

"She finally broke down and confided everything to me. The image that Ted showed us wasn't really him. It was a ploy to get Rebecca. And once he had her, he threatened to do to me what he was doing to her if she left."

Rachel glanced over at Asher to find him sitting very still as he listened. There was no pity on his face, just anger and revulsion for what Ted had done.

She flattened her hands together, rubbing them to help bring back some warmth. "I convinced Rebecca to tell my parents everything, and we came together as a family again. I stood by as my sister called Ted and told him it was over, that we all knew what he really was. Meanwhile, my parents called the sheriff, who was a friend. He met us at the station where Rebecca filed a restraining order against Ted."

"A piece of paper is nothing to men like him," Asher stated.

"It was her only step to take. We thought it would give us time. And for two weeks, it did. Rebecca was slowly returning to her old self." She turned the thumb ring over and over. "The night of my birthday, she gave me this ring. We celebrated as a family. It was a truly wonderful night. We had suffered and got through a horrendous time.

"In the early hours of that morning, our house caught fire. Rebecca dragged me from my room, but I passed out from smoke inhalation. I didn't learn until I woke in the hospital that the fire started in my parents' room. On their bed."

She had to stop and close her eyes. It had been so long since she thought of the way that her parents had so brutally died, that her stomach rolled.

"You doona have to finish."

She shook her head and continued. "Ted broke into our house and set my parents on fire. The house was soon ablaze. He went after Rebecca, but she managed to evade him long enough to get to me. Since I was unconscious, I slowed her down. Ted killed her with a shot to the back of the head. I think he expected me to die in the blaze, but the firefighters got there in time."

"You saw Ted?"

"No, but I knew it was him. When the police told me how my parents and sister died, there could be no one else. He had probable cause and motivation."

Asher nodded slowly.

"Thanks to the photos taken at the police station and Rebecca's statement along with the restraining order, the police went after him. That's when the truth of Ted Montgomery came out." She turned her head to Asher. "You see, Rebecca and my parents weren't his first victims. He'd done this before, but he came from money and his father managed to pay off people to cover his son's crimes. Had someone exposed the truth of him from the beginning, Rebecca and my parents would still be alive."

"I'm verra sorry for what you've endured. You're right. It was a senseless tragedy."

She drew in a shaky breath and took another drink of wine. The retelling had taken a lot out of her, but there was a small measure of triumph for knowing Ted was behind bars for the rest of his life. No other family would be hurt by him.

"That's not a story I wanted to tell you tonight," she said and forced a smile.

"It's part of who you are, lass. Why wouldna I want to know?"

"We barely know each other."

His green eyes held hers. "This is how we remedy that. I, too, lost my family."

She held her breath, uncertain that she wanted to hear this. Already she was finding it harder and harder to do her job. If she connected with

Asher any more, she might walk away from it altogether.

And she wasn't entirely sure what Sam MacDonald might do if she did.

"My father was a soldier. He died in battle," Asher explained.

It was on the tip of her tongue to ask which battle, but she remained silent.

"My mother was inconsolable. My siblings and I did what we could, but nothing replaces a mate of the soul. My eldest sister married and had children of her own, and my two younger brothers followed in my father's footsteps."

"But not you?"

He looked down at his nearly empty whisky glass. "My path was different. I was a soldier of sorts myself. I was thrust into a position that I had wanted for a long time. I stepped into the role willingly, only to learn that it would eventually rule my life."

She didn't move a muscle. She was even afraid to breathe lest he stop talking. She wasn't sure how much he would share, and part of her didn't want to know anything. The more she knew, the more she would have to share with the world. It was the oath she gave herself when her family was murdered. She couldn't go back on that now—for anybody.

His green eyes swung to her. "My mother died of heartbreak six months later, and to my utter astonishment, I had to send the rest of my family away."

"Away?" she asked, frowning.

"In order to keep them safe, so they might live." He tossed back the last of his whisky. "Let me tell you a story, Rae. It starts with the creation of this planet."

Chapter Eleven

Asher watched as Rae's face paled. She was physically shaken from sharing the story of her tragedy. That wasn't faked. Of that he was certain.

Nor was her reaction to his statement.

He remained in his relaxed position—when he was anything but. She had intentionally deceived him. There would be a price paid for that. For now, however, it was time for his story.

After all, she knew what he was.

Before he'd gone down to the bar, Ryder had contacted him through their link. Thanks to Ryder's ability to ferret out all information, he found a connection between Rae—Rachel—and Ulrik, with his alias of Sam MacDonald.

It hadn't been easy, because Ulrik covered his tracks so well, but Ryder was that fucking good. Though it didn't make hearing the news any easier.

He wished he had more whisky. It would take an entire case to get him through this night. He'd wanted Rae to be who he thought she was last night. Not who Ms. Engel and Ryder uncovered.

He wanted her to be special. To be…his.

That was looking more and more impossible.

"This realm is billions of years old," he began. "For a large portion of it, there were no humans. Only dragons."

If it was possible, her face paled even more. Her hands clasped together and she glanced at the door.

He wasn't about to let her escape. Not until he told his side of the story. "Dragons no bigger than a house cat and larger than you could possibly imagine. The dragons were separated by colors, and the strongest of that color was their king. But the most powerful of all the dragons was King of Kings. During this time, the dragons roamed the sky, the land,

and the seas, ruling over everything. Until one day mortals arrived."

Rae didn't beg him to stop or try to change the subject. A small frown puckered her forehead as she listened. And that was enough for him.

"The day the humans arrived, each Dragon King suddenly found themselves in human form. We didn't know how, but it allowed us to communicate with the mortals. From then on, we were able to shift from dragon to human at will."

The fact she didn't seemed fazed by his words affirmed that Ulrik had indeed told her who Asher was. This was a new tactic from Ulrik, but one they should've expected.

He drew in a deep breath and released it. "We made room for the humans, giving them land dragons had occupied for thousands of years. But the mortals multiplied at an astonishing rate. They demanded more and more land, pushing dragons out of their homes and causing friction.

"Despite all of this, many humans found it beneficial to be near a King for protection. Females sought us out as lovers. It went on like that for years until one of us decided to take his lover as his mate, or wife."

"And how was this wrong?" Rae asked.

"Dragons mate for life. Unlike mortals. This Dragon King was the best of us. Ulrik was kind and always had a smile. He loved to play jokes, but there was none more loyal. He could've been King of Kings."

She shook her head in confusion. "Then why didn't he?"

"Because he was happy being a King to his Silvers. His best friend was King of Kings, and in order to gain the title, he would have to kill Constantine."

At the mention of Con, her mouth went slack.

So she knew of Con as well, but obviously not all of it. He continued. "Ulrik believed his woman loved him as deeply as he did her. Days before their mating, Con discovered Ulrik's woman sought to betray him. Con knew how deeply it would hurt Ulrik, and that Ulrik would feel he had to punish her. Con sought to save his friend such a horror and sent him on a mission. Then Con called all the Kings together and told us what he'd learned.

"Each of us became enraged for Ulrik and because this mortal would dare to betray one of us. We chased her down and killed her."

Rae's eyes widened, her body becoming so still Asher couldn't see her breathing. "What kind of betrayal warranted such a reaction?"

"She was going to kill Ulrik."

Her face crumpled into confusion. "Why? Ulrik was protecting her, loving her?"

"Why does anyone betray another? This mortal used Ulrik to get close to him. She wanted to start a war between the dragons and humans. Unbeknownst to her, only another Dragon King can kill one of us. Nothing she could've tried would've worked to end Ulrik's life."

Rae's shoulders sagged. "But had she succeeded, Ulrik would've endured firsthand her betrayal."

"Aye. We protected him and attempted to stop a war. Except it didna work. Ulrik returned and discovered what we did. He felt betrayed by his lover—and us."

"You were helping him."

Asher nodded. "It didna matter. He was engulfed with grief and rage. It was a horrendous combination for one such as him. He couldna control it, and with his Silvers, he began to attack the human settlements. The rest of the Kings went into action, either setting up our dragons as protection against Ulrik or attempting to stop him.

"The real heartbreak occurred when the mortals turned on the verra dragons protecting them. The dragons had orders to safeguard the humans, so they didna defend themselves. Dragons were slaughtered everywhere. And that divided the Kings. Many joined Ulrik, intending to wipe the mortals from our realm for good."

"What side were you on?"

Asher thought back to his Hunters. Such magnificent creatures his dragons were. "I happened to be returning to a village where my dragons stood guard. I saw the humans attacking and killing them. And I released my dragons from their obligation, which allowed them to shield themselves. I didna join Ulrik, but I thought about it after watching what the mortals did to my dragons.

"Con proved why he was King of Kings and eventually won back the Kings to his side. But Ulrik wouldna stop killing. No dragon was safe. The humans wanted us gone. They wouldna talk to us of a truce or come to some sort of agreement."

She turned more toward him. "I don't understand. You're dragons. You could've easily wiped them out."

"We made a vow the day the first human arrived to protect your kind with our verra lives. We have magic and powers. The majority of mortals doona. That vow extended to us as well. When several of the smaller dragons were hunted to extinction, we did the only thing we could. We sent the dragons away to another realm."

"Including Ulrik's Silvers?" she asked.

"All but his largest four. They remained with him, refusing to answer to Con. We managed to trap them however. They've been sleeping within one of the mountains on Dreagan since then."

She blinked, her face filled with concern. "Trapped?"

"No' even that stopped Ulrik. It took us banishing him from Dreagan, binding his magic so he had to walk this earth as a human for all eternity."

"You banished one of your own?"

"It was either that or kill him. Con didna want to kill his best friend."

Rae gave a snort. "I think I'd rather die than walk around the very beings I sought to exterminate."

"Aye. He detests mortals. But no' even the extremes we went to in order to protect the humans changed their minds about us. We had no choice but to hide on Dreagan, using magic to ensure no mortal would take the land while we slept. We waited hundreds of years before we began to once more venture out. By then, dragons were mere legends and myths.

"For thousands of years we watched Ulrik as we kept ourselves secret. Recently, he has begun attacking us, and once more setting in motion another dragon and human war. Ulrik found a Druid who could touch dragon magic."

"Wait, what?" Rae asked with a bark of laughter. "A Druid?"

"You didna believe me when I said there were some mortals with magic? The Druids are real and extremely powerful. This Druid was deceived by Ulrik into unbinding his magic."

She gawked at him. "If Ulrik's magic has returned, what's to stop him from releasing his Silvers?"

"Nothing. We know he plans on doing just that, and we're attempting to stop him. It doesna help that he has some humans, as well as Dark Fae, helping him. It was the Dark who took that video of us during the battle at Dreagan."

"Dark Fae?" she asked in a tight voice.

Asher released a breath. "We vowed to protect you from everything, and there is a lot of things out in the universe. The Dark Fae were the ones causing such havoc in the cities around the UK during Halloween. They have black and silver hair with red eyes. You humans are drawn to them, but each time they have sex with you, they drain you of your soul."

"Are there Light Fae?"

"Aye. They joined with us when we fought the Dark during the Fae Wars when the Dark attempted to take over this realm so every human could be a food source."

She turned her head away, the truth of it all troubling her. "Fae Wars?"

"It was a long time ago, and we managed to keep the war from spreading to the mortals. With the way humans cover so much of the planet now, that willna be possible. Besides, Ulrik is already bringing you into the war without you realizing it."

"But Ulrik hates us."

Asher smiled sadly. "More than you can possibly imagine. Your race is the reason he lost his dragons, his magic, and was banished. But he blames us as well. His goal is to defeat Con and take over as King of Kings."

"Which will mean the end of humans."

"That it will."

She visibly swallowed. "Why did you tell me all of this?"

"Because you were given half of the information."

Her face went slack as it finally dawned on her. "You know."

"You mean do I know that Rae and Rachel Marek are the same? Aye. You mean do I know that you've been following me around the WWC masking your appearance? Aye. You mean, do I know that you're a journalist who has made a career out of exposing cover-ups, imposters, cheats, and such to the world? Aye."

He had to give her credit, she didn't bolt to the door. There was fear in her deep brown eyes as she returned his stare, but she kept herself composed.

She lifted her chin. "I was told that though the Dragon Kings tended to seduce women, they could turn on them."

"Did you no' hear anything I just told you?" he asked, disgusted. "We made a fucking vow. We sacrificed our families in order to protect your species. Why would we kill you? We could've done that thousands of years ago and none of this would be happening now."

When she didn't reply, he shoved to his feet and raked a hand through his hair. "The sad part is how you unknowingly picked a side in this war."

"The only side I've chosen is my own. The world deserves to know you're here."

"What about our rights? Have you thought of that?"

She refused to respond, which only frustrated him.

"Did you know that Ulrik has made it his mission to go after every female a King has taken an interest in?" He didn't wait for her to answer before continuing. "When I say he's gone after them, I mean he's either had the Dark kidnap them or attempted to kill them. We were lucky with the Dark. We have a Light friend who risked her life to help us."

"And the attempted murder?"

He raked a hand through his hair again as he thought of the women. "There were two. Ulrik turned Lily's brother against her. He killed her. I stood watching as Rhys held her in his arms as her life drained away."

"I...I don't understand. You said attempted."

"For reasons we can no' understand, Ulrik brought her back."

"Excuse me?" she asked in disbelief.

He shrugged. "We each have a power. Con can heal anything. Ulrik can bring a person back from the dead."

"So he brought Lily back? Seems like he's not so bad."

"There's a reason he did it. We've no' figured it out yet."

She glanced out the window and grudgingly asked, "And the second?"

"The Druid I told you about—Darcy. He stabbed her. It was only the quick actions of Druids who saved her."

"It seems since I have a connection to you that I should know what this Ulrik looks like."

Asher smiled ruefully. "You already do. You know him as Sam MacDonald."

Chapter Twelve

Rachel couldn't have been more shocked if Asher had told her Ms. Engel was a dragon. She could only stare at him as she fought to drag air into her lungs. The room tilted and she grabbed hold of the sofa to keep herself righted. Sam was Ulrik. Sam. Was Ulrik.

No. That couldn't be possible.

But it explained why he knew so much about the Dragon Kings. It explained how he'd gotten the information and drawn Asher to such detail.

Oh God. She was going to be sick.

Something was placed in her hand, and then Asher's voice ordered, "Drink, Rae. Drink now."

She lifted the glass to her lips and took a big swallow. Then promptly coughed as the whisky burned down her throat before spreading its warmth when it hit her stomach.

Her eyes watered from the coughing, or at least that's what she told herself. All her life she'd made it her mission to expose the wrong kinds of people, but she'd been used and duped as she swore she'd never let happen again.

It felt horrible, and the anger that bubbled within her was powerful. What an utter fool she must look like in Asher's eyes. All that time being so confident that she had been able to be both places without him knowing it was her.

"Finish it," he urged and pushed the glass to her mouth once more.

This time she took a much smaller sip. She then put the back of her hand over her mouth and squeezed her eyes shut. All it had taken was Ulrik's words and the video to convince her to look into the Dragon

Kings—that is, after her initial freaked out reaction to knowing there was another species on the earth.

Then she turned everything she had on exposing them.

Now she learned there were Druids and Fae as well. Dark Fae who killed by sex. She coughed, gagging a little as she realized she had chosen a side, just as Asher said.

The sofa dipped as he sat beside her. "Look at me."

She inhaled deeply, dropping her arm as she opened her eyes while turning her head to him. A lock of black hair had fallen over his forehead ever since he ran his hand through his hair. In his green gaze she saw concern.

How could he care for her after what she had been about to do? Then she recalled his words. Everything she'd learned about Asher in the days following him, talking to him, and even making love to him, pointed to him being a good man.

It had killed her to admit it before, but now that she heard his story and knew who Sam was, she was glad of it.

"How long have you known?" she asked.

He twisted his lips. "Today. I noticed your thumb ring as well as someone I kept seeing at the WWC with the same ring, just on a different hand."

She twisted the ring. "What happens now?"

He tucked a strand of her hair behind her ear. "That depends on you. Ulrik normally waits until a King has shown interest in a woman before he tries to either turn her against the King or kill her in some way."

"Now it makes sense," she said, shaking her head wryly.

He frowned. "What does?"

"Sam asked me if I would fall for you. I told him that wouldn't be a problem since I didn't feel desire."

"At all?" Asher asked, his frown deepening.

"Never. Until you."

The frown was replaced with a grin. But that lasted only a second before worry contorted his features. "Are you still going to write your piece?"

"I don't think you should be hiding. I think eventually it's all going to come out. But I won't be the one to tell the world." She didn't know when she'd come to that conclusion. Perhaps it was during his story. It might have been when he forced her to think of him and the other Dragon Kings and what they wanted.

"Then I can help you. Have you spoken to Ulrik since you've been in

Paris?"

She gave a shake of her head, comforted when Asher's hand covered hers on her leg. "He told me he was going to be at Dreagan. I've never not written a story, so he fully expects me to gather as much information on you as I can and then write my article to be released a week or two later."

"If we doona have to worry about you answering to him, that helps. However, I wouldna put it past Ulrik to have you watched."

"Why?"

"To make sure you doona fall for me."

She couldn't hold his gaze. She looked at their hands atop her lap and thought of what she wanted. Without a doubt, she wanted Asher.

That thought brought her up short.

Did she really want him in her life? She couldn't believe that she did. Because of her lack of passion, she had never understood relationships or wanting her space invaded by someone else. Now she got it.

"How do I untangle myself from Sam...I mean Ulrik?"

He squeezed her hand. "You're going to have to trust me, lass."

Her gaze swung back to him. "I trusted Sam or Ulrik or whoever he is. My judgment is skewed right now."

"No it isna. Ulrik gave you information you needed in order to agree to write the piece and have something else besides the video exposing us."

"Anyone could write an article. Why did he choose me?"

"Because your name is synonymous with the truth. Having you linked to it would make it valid and hard for us to disclaim as fake like we do the video."

She blew out a breath. "I hate how this makes me feel."

"That makes two of us."

She ran her thumb of his hand. "You could've walked away and never spoken to me again. I wouldn't have gotten anything more from you."

"I could've, but I didna want to."

"Why?"

There was a pause before he said, "You're special. To me."

Her heart missed a beat. Last night had been extraordinary for her, but she assumed it was one sided. Could he feel the same? She grinned at him and felt her stomach quiver in anticipation when he returned her smile.

"I doona think you got much from me before tonight, did you?"

She laughed as she shook her head. "I tried. I kept telling myself to steer the conversation that way, but for some reason I couldn't."

"Good."

When he leaned back and drew her against his chest, she readily went. It felt nice to be in his arms and know that he would watch over her. Not because of a vow he made to all humans, but because he had told her he would.

"What if Ulrik is having me watched?" she asked.

"The only way you'll be completely safe from him is to write the article."

"But I don't want to now."

Asher's chest expanded as he took a breath. "He'll no' accept that you've changed your mind."

She recalled how he'd gotten into her hotel room in London with the door bolted. "No. That he won't."

"His connections are far and deep. You wouldna ever be able to hide from him."

"My options are running out quickly."

He rested his chin atop her head. "There is a place where he wouldna be able to hurt you."

"Where? Dreagan?" she asked jokingly.

"Aye."

She leaned back to look at him and saw the seriousness in his expression. "You're not kidding."

"Nay, I'm no'."

A thread of exhilaration rushed through her at the thought of exploring Dreagan, seeing how Asher lived, and possibly glimpsing the Silvers. Then she imagined seeing him in his dragon form.

Suddenly, it was the only thing she wanted.

"I can keep you safe," Asher offered.

"Out of obligation from your vow when we humans first came?"

He grasped the back of her head and kissed her savagely. She could taste and feel his hunger. Passion roared to life within her as she eagerly returned his kiss. She groaned in frustration when he ended it. Her eyes blinked as she focused on his face.

"Did that feel like obligation?" he asked, his voice rough with desire.

She shook her head, unable to talk.

"I want you with me."

She kicked off her shoes and pulled up her dress so she could straddle his hips. "Show me."

His gradual smile was so sexy it made her moan. He grasped a handful of her hair and held her head in place as he kissed her slowly, seductively. Between kisses he pledged, "I'll make you burn again."

The fever for him, for everything he was, consumed her as his hand cupped her sex through her panties.

Chapter Thirteen

The next morning, Asher met Ms. Engel in the lobby. As they got into the car, he said, "Excellent work on discovering who Rachel really is."

"Thank you, sir."

"I need you to keep an eye on her for me."

Ms. Engel gave a nod of her dark hair. "Consider it done."

"There could be some people after her."

Her head snapped to him. "That kind of trouble?"

"Unfortunately. I must keep to my schedule."

"Yes," she said slowly, her gaze lowering to the floorboard as her mind began to work. "There is a group that can be trusted. But they aren't cheap."

He didn't want to call in outsiders, but if another Dragon King arrived, it would alert Ulrik, and that was something he wanted to avoid. Enough innocents had already died.

Not to mention, Dreagan didn't need any more attention.

"I've worked with them numerous times," Ms. Engel said. "They'll keep their mouths shut about anything they might...see."

She all but confirmed that she knew they were dragons. Just how, though? It was something he would have to ask Con. But that was for later. Right now, there were more pressing matters.

"I doona have a choice." Asher looked out the tinted window and sighed. After a moment, he turned his head to Ms. Engel. "Call them. I want to know who she talks to, who looks at her, and where she goes."

Immediately, she pulled out her phone and hit a single number before lifting it to her ear while she flipped the case to her tablet and opened an e-mail. Typing, she said, "I have a Code White. Yes. Right away. I'm sending the specifics as we speak." She hit the send button on the e-mail and hung up the phone. Her gaze shifted to Asher. "It's done. They'll be at the hotel within fifteen minutes. If anything happens, they'll contact me."

"Make sure they know that if a man with long black hair and gold eyes is seen that he is mine."

"Of course."

They arrived at the exhibition centre. Asher exited the car and made his way inside. He covertly searched for any sign that Ulrik was there. As much as he wanted to believe that Ulrik was in Scotland, Ulrik wasn't one to leave things to fate. He would want to check on Rachel's progress. Which meant the bastard was there.

There was a push against his mind as he sat down for his next meeting. He recognized Con's voice and opened the link. "*Aye?*"

"*Ryder told me about Rachel Marek. Is everything under control?*"

"*For the moment.*"

There was a sigh loud enough to come through the mental link. "*You told her.*"

It wasn't a question. "*Aye. She believed the load of shite Ulrik gave her, and she was still going to write the article. She needed the truth.*"

"*Perhaps. But now you've only put her life in jeopardy because Ulrik will learn what you've done. Especially when she doesna write the article.*"

"*Aye.*"

There was a lengthy pause before Constantine stated in a hard voice, "*You're bringing her to Dreagan.*"

"*I'll no' leave her for Ulrik to kill, which we both know he will. Either he'll kill her or threaten her enough so she writes the article, then he kills her. That willna happen.*"

"*So you've fallen for her?*"

"*She was lied to, and her life is in danger. I'm doing what needs to be done.*"

Con then said, "*There are places she could go. The Isle of Skye for one. The Druids would watch her. Better yet, send her to MacLeod Castle. The Warriors and Druids will protect her.*"

Those were viable options, but Asher wanted no part in them. "*This is our mess. We'll do the protecting."*

"Are none of you concerned with how many are finding mates? No' even before the spell we cast on ourselves no' to have such feelings for the mortals we didna have so many mates."

"Maybe this is our curse for going all those centuries without such feelings. It does concern me, because the more mates we have, the more we have to protect, and the more Ulrik can hurt us. But none of that changes the fact Rachel will be returning with me."

"And you believe she's no longer working with Ulrik? You trust that she has turned her back on that?"

"Aye."

"Then bring her home."

The link was disconnected, and Asher returned to focusing on the meeting.

* * * *

Rachel stretched beneath the covers and smiled. Sunlight filtered through the curtains and filled the room. Asher's room. She had spent another wonderful night with him.

She rolled over to his pillow and found a deep purple calla lily upon it with a note. Rachel picked up the note, noticing the elegantly neat script.

No more hiding. Join me today.

Yours,
A

She tucked the note to her chest and held the flower. After reading the note a few more times, she rose and dressed to return to her room.

Asher was right. She was done hiding. The confessions and revelations last night had wiped away any need for that. Excitement pumped through her at being her real self with him. It was the side of her she hadn't known was even there, but he made it shine.

She quite liked this new her. It was certainly going to make it difficult for her to continue her work in the manner that she had. If she could continue.

Once inside her room, she checked every space and turned on the water for the shower. Sam, or rather Ulrik, wasn't going to be happy about her change of heart. She also agreed with Asher that Ulrik might come after her.

There were still ways to expose the truth of others to the world. Except now, she would dig even deeper than before. Nothing she learned about Asher or Dreagan would've given her the story she heard last night.

She stepped into the shower and wondered what might've happened had he not told her and she wrote the story. What those words—while true—could've destroyed?

What *had* her words destroyed?

She winced as she thought about all the people and companies she had exposed in the course of telling the truth. Had families been ripped apart? Had they suffered? Though she tried not to think of it, the thought was already there.

If she announced the truth, people got hurt.

If she didn't share what she knew, people got hurt.

How was she ever going to know what was the right thing to do now?

She turned on some music to drown out her mind and dressed. She chose a pair of black jeans, a black sweater, and the camel-colored long coat. Tall black boots would keep her feet warm. She opted to put her hair up in a messy side bun with her diamond stud earrings, the locket with pictures of her family, and her thumb ring.

After a look at the flower, Rachel walked from the room. On her way out of the lobby, someone called her name. She turned and found one of the concierges rushing toward her.

The man said, "*Mademoiselle*, I just sent a bellman up to your room to let you know I have a message."

"Message?" she asked, suddenly wary.

"*Oui.* He said he didn't have much time, but asked that you meet him at this address."

Rachel accepted the paper with a smile. "Thank you."

"*Au Revoir.*"

"*Au Revoir,*" she replied as she looked at the address. Why hadn't Asher called her? Though she didn't give him her mobile number, he'd learned everything else.

She adjusted her purse on her shoulder and walked outside to the waiting taxi. Once inside the car, she handed the paper to the driver. "I'd like to go here, please."

The driver, a man with wide-set eyes, a large nose, and a rather wide bald spot at the back of his head eyed the paper then her. "Are you sure?" he asked in a heavy French accent.

"*Oui.*"

With a shrug, he drove away from the hotel. Rachel checked her texts and her e-mails, but there was nothing from Sam/Ulrik. There hadn't been before either. But Asher had her worried. Since learning what Sam/Ulrik was capable of, she had reason to be apprehensive of him.

Thank God she was with Asher. She still couldn't believe he wanted to help guard her against Sam/Ulrik, but she was going to accept it. Somehow, she would make it up to him and the rest of the Dragon Kings for what she had nearly done.

She put the phone away and looked up. Only to frown. Gone was the beautiful architecture of the Paris she knew. This was the section of the city no tourist ever saw. Surely this couldn't be where Asher wanted to meet.

The taxi pulled over. She craned her head to look out the window at what was left of the crumbling, rusted warehouse. There wasn't a single window that wasn't broken, and the door, tilted and hanging by one hinge, stood half-open.

"This isn't a good place for you to be."

She jerked at the driver's voice, having forgotten she wasn't alone. She glanced at him. Asher wouldn't have sent for her if it weren't important.

With her resolve in place, she paid her fare and opened the car door.

"Should I stay?" the driver asked.

Rachel opened her mouth to tell him "yes" when she spotted the front of the Jaguar parked on the other side of the warehouse. "Thank you, but no. I've got a ride back."

She watched the taxi drive off with the man still shaking his head inside. She sucked in a breath as a gust of frigid wind slammed into her. Turning on her heel, she strode to the door where she saw the chain swinging around the door handle. It was still bright silver, it was so new. Obviously Asher had a key to get in the place.

The metal door was ice cold against her palm. When she pushed against it, the door emitted a loud squeak that had her jerking her hand back. She shook her head, smiling. She didn't scare easily, but knowing someone like Ulrik was out there had obviously unsettled her more than she realized.

She tucked her purse against her front and squeezed through the opening. Inside the warehouse she blinked against the darkness while her eyes adjusted. It smelled musty and old, the unuse evident in the clutter and debris that littered the floor. Her heels were loud on the concrete as she took slow, uncertain steps.

A flurry off to her left alarmed her as pigeons, startled from their slumber, flew to the upper recesses of the building. She followed their flight to see just how huge the warehouse was.

Perhaps big enough for a dragon.

Could that be why Asher had called her here? She hoped it was. She knew so much about him now, but she didn't know that part. And she was anxious to see him.

"Asher," she called softly. Then louder, she said, "Asher!"

Chapter Fourteen

The door opened to the meeting room, and Asher's gaze immediately shifted to see who it was. The instant he saw Ms. Engel, he knew. Without a word to the others in attendance, Asher pushed back his chair and strode toward the door where she waited.

Outside of the room in the nearly deserted corridor, he turned and asked, "What happened?"

"It appears someone sent Rachel to a deserted warehouse."

Asher pivoted and lengthened his strides as he made his way to the front of the building where his car awaited. Several people called his name, but he didn't glance their way.

His main thought—his *only* thought—was getting to Rachel in time. It would be so much easier if he could shift and fly to her. He could be there in seconds. Instead, he had to take the mortal route by car. Through traffic. Red lights. Stop signs.

And people.

It was almost too much to bear.

It wasn't until they were in the car that Ms. Engel said, "An address was given to her at the hotel. One of the men said the hotel staff gave it to her, claiming it came from a call. They never used a name. She must've assumed it was from you."

He squeezed his eyes closed. "I told her to join me at the WWC."

"I see."

He pinched the bridge of his nose with his thumb and forefinger before he opened his eyes. "Are the people you hired at the warehouse?"

"Yes. There are four of them."

Their numbers didn't matter if Ulrik was involved. "Did they see anyone with Rachel?"

"When I was contacted, they were attempting to gain access into the building where she went."

"Call them off. Now," he barked.

Without question, she grabbed her phone and sent two numbers in a text. "They'll wait for your arrival."

As the minutes ticked by with agonizing slowness, he thought of all the ways Ulrik could hurt Rachel.

And then he thought of all the ways he was going to kill Ulrik.

None of it alleviated his fear. If anything, it made it double until he was choking on it. He should never have left her alone. She had been sleeping so soundly that he hadn't wanted to wake her. If only he had. They wouldn't be in this mess. Then again, if it wasn't today, it would've been another day.

This scenario would've played out one way or another.

He hated to acknowledge that, but there it was. Nothing a Dragon King did could completely safeguard a mate. For all their immortality, power, and magic, the Kings had too much to lose to fight Ulrik as they should.

It was never more clear than at that moment what lengths Ulrik would go to in order to achieve his goal. And it was never clearer what the Kings needed to do in order to win.

Con wasn't going to like it, but Ulrik was backing them into a very tight corner. Their choices were quickly dwindling.

As soon as they turned down the street lined with old buildings, many abandoned, Asher ordered the driver to stop. From the inside of the car, he took stock of his surroundings.

The warehouses were tall and numerous, leaving ample room for Ulrik to hide among any of them. It was a trap. Plain and simple. He was prepared for it, but Rachel wasn't. None of the humans were. Because he wasn't certain if Ulrik had brought mortals—or Dark Fae.

"Which building is it?" he asked Ms. Engel.

She laid her arm between the front seats and pointed out the windshield. "The third on the right."

He looked from the driver to her. "Thank you both. When I get out, I want you to back up and drive away."

"Sir," Ms. Engel protested.

He held up a hand. "Call off the people watching Rachel. I want everyone gone."

"You might need help," she protested.

"It'll be better if there were no witnesses to what I'm about to do. Nor do I want any of you to get hurt."

He reached for the door when her hand grasped his wrist. Asher turned his head toward her.

Ms. Engel's face was filled with apprehension as she stared at him through her glasses. "Be careful, sir."

"Worry about those attempting to hurt Rachel, Ms. Engel," he declared and climbed out of the car.

He shut the door, and just as he ordered, they backed up and drove away. He waited several tense minutes to be sure the people watching Rachel had time to get away.

Then he began walking to the warehouse.

* * * *

Rachel felt a shiver glide down her spine like the fingers of the dead. If Asher were here, he would've shown himself. This was wrong, all wrong.

She took a step back and felt the heel of her boot sink into something. Glancing down, she saw she had stepped into the carcass of a decomposing rat. She gagged and swiftly moved to the side.

The rat was soon forgotten as the hairs on the back of her neck rose. She stilled, her gaze moving around the shadow-filled warehouse to see who was watching her. That was enough. She turned to retrace her steps to the door. It didn't matter if she had to walk back to the hotel, she wasn't remaining there an instant longer.

She was about to pass through a darkened area she had just been through moments before when her feet halted. Though she couldn't see into the dark, she knew someone—or something—was there.

When she took a step back, something moved in the darkness. Unable to stop herself, she took another step back.

Her heart leapt into her throat when she saw a pair of eyes shining in the dark move toward her. A face took shape, a gorgeous male face with a mocking smile and evil red eyes.

"What a tasty morsel," he said in an Irish accent.

Dark Fae. She backed up another step, only to bump into someone. She didn't turn around to see who it was. There was no need to see more of the beautiful horror that was before her.

"Cat got your tongue?" asked the male voice behind her.

Another Irishman. Her heart fell to her feet. The man before her moved closer and she saw his chin-length hair, more silver than black.

There wasn't the overwhelming need to have sex with them as Asher said, but that could be because she was in the cold grip of fear. Apparently the Dark was thinking the same thing as he frowned.

"What's wrong with you?" he demanded, anger tingeing his words.

"She's been with a Dragon King."

The third male voice came from her left, and there was no mistaking the Scottish brogue. It wasn't Asher's voice, yet Rachel recognized it somehow.

The man behind her laid his hands on her shoulders heavily and squeezed hard. "I don't care who she's been with. I want her."

"Not before I've had a go at her," stated the first Irishman.

The Scotsman remained in the shadows, but whatever he did shut the two Irishmen up. "It's really too bad that you didna complete what you were sent here to do, Rachel."

"I'm still working on it," she lied.

The laugh that followed was hollow. "You fell for the Dragon King. The one thing you promised you wouldna do."

Sam. Rachel inwardly gasped when she realized why she recognized the voice. It was Sam/Ulrik standing before her. Gone was the cultured British accent. Now he was revealing who he really was.

"Nothing to say?" Ulrik asked sarcastically.

She gave a shake of her head. "It wouldn't matter what I said. You've already condemned me."

"Tell me what you've learned."

"I don't know you. I'm not telling you anything." Thank God her voice came out more confident than she felt.

Because she realized just what kind of precarious position she was in without anyone to save her. How stupid to assume it was Asher who sent for her to such a place. This proved how naïve she still was about so many things despite uncovering as much garbage as she did on a daily basis.

She honestly thought she had time before Ulrik came for her. She foolishly assumed that he would do as he said and allow her to work. Asher had known. He'd told her Ulrik would be watching. She should've remembered that when she so happily went off to meet him at a rundown warehouse.

What an asinine way to die—by stupidity.

"I detest betrayal. There is no coming back from this."

She released a shuddering breath. It was obvious that to Ulrik a betrayal of any kind meant death. Now that she knew his story, she understood. But that didn't mean she agreed with it.

"What did Asher tell you?" Ulrik demanded.

If she was going to die, then she was going out swinging. "Step into the light. Let me see your face."

"This is about you, no' me."

"You brought me here. Reveal yourself. Or are you afraid of what I might tell the world when I discover who you are?"

"You want to know me?" he threatened in a voice laced with a promise of violence.

She locked her knees. It was the only way she could remain standing, she was so frightened. "I already know you, don't I? Ulrik."

His laugh, a harsh sound between malevolence and indifference, made even the two Dark Fae take a step back from her—and him.

"Just what do you think you know, little mortal? That wee bit of information Asher imparted means nothing," Ulrik stated in a calm voice.

Which only fed her fear.

She had known Sam was dangerous, but she hadn't realized just how much until she learned his true identity. Even then, she had arrogantly thought she could handle things.

He was a Dragon King. A fucking real-life being with powers and magic and the ability to breathe fire. She was a mere speck of dirt on the bottom of his foot.

Little mortal? He let it be known just how inconsequential she was to the outcome of whatever he had planned.

All those top executives and corporations with international reaches never scared her no matter how much they threatened. She knew her rights as a journalist, and knew just how far she could push to get the information she needed.

None of that mattered when dealing with a pissed off banished Dragon King with vengeance on his mind. With a flick of his finger, he could end her life.

She no longer worried about the Dark. Her sole focus was Ulrik, who remained in the shadows. She knew what he looked like, knew the shrewdness she'd seen in his cold golden eyes.

Ulrik turned out to be exactly what she had been fighting against by revealing others' true forms. That same awful feeling of betrayal filled her. It was something she swore to never experience again. It was as if Ulrik had known how to exploit her weakness, and he'd done it with taciturn finality.

"You used me in your war against the Kings," she stated.

Though she couldn't see him, she could feel him shrug. "Shite happens. Is that no' what you humans say?"

"Wouldn't you know? You've walked among us for thousands of years. You had to live in a human's body while only imagining being your true self once more."

She wasn't sure where those words had come from. Panic had an iron grip on her, but the anger churning within her swelled and spread. Overriding common sense and putting her right in his crosshairs.

Not that she hadn't been there just a second before.

Ulrik's only response was another hollow chuckle that sent ice through her veins.

Chapter Fifteen

Asher removed his jacket, shoes, and socks before he entered the warehouse. He wanted nothing to come between his feet and the ground. No slippery sole, no squeak of leather.

Once inside the building, he was able to hear the conversation more clearly. Two Dark were there, though he expected there was a chance more were waiting.

Good.

He wanted the chance to release some of the rage suffocating him. He fought against shifting right then. It would give him an advantage over Ulrik, at least he hoped. They knew from Darcy that some of Ulrik's magic had been unbound, but the Druid didn't know if all of it had been. The Kings assumed it hadn't since Ulrik had yet to shift or release his dragons.

If he had all his magic, he could easily free his Silvers and start up the war again. More importantly, he could shift and confirm that dragons were real.

He hadn't done either. That made Asher pause. Ulrik was one of the most cunning of the Kings. It would be just like him to allow the Kings to think he didn't have all his magic, when in fact he did.

Then he thought of the confrontation between Con and Ulrik not that long ago. They fought, and it would've been the perfect time for Ulrik to challenge Con for the right to be King of Kings.

But Ulrik hadn't. No way would he have let that chance fall into his lap and not grasp it if he had all his magic.

He crept closer to the group. Ulrik and the Dark had Rachel cornered. First thing he needed to do was get rid of the Dark. Those filthy beings had no place near his woman.

Broken glass sank into the bottom of his feet, but he didn't register the pain. His concentration was riveted on the small group. Though he hadn't had direct contact with Ulrik since before he was banished, he wasn't prepared for the change in Ulrik's voice.

The hatred was thick, coating his words with revulsion and disgust. Asher didn't need to look into his eyes to know there wouldn't be an ounce of mercy. Whatever kindness and compassion used to be in Ulrik had long since become extinct. The only things that resided within him were callousness and retribution.

He heard Rachel's voice shake even as she stood up to Ulrik. That took a lot of nerve considering it was Ulrik. He would have to applaud her later, right after he gave her a little shake for irritating their enemy so.

The Dark didn't like Ulrik's tone. They continued to step away from him and Rachel. Asher veered to come up behind one of the Dark.

He covered the Dark's mouth with one hand before yanking the Dark's heart out with the other. He didn't drop him as he wanted to do. Instead, Asher quietly lowered the body to the floor and placed the heart next to it.

Then he turned his attention to the other Fae. Soundlessly, he snuck up behind the remaining Dark Fae. Just as he was about to grab him, the Dark turned, eyes going wide as he spotted Asher.

He dodged a hastily thrown ball of magic and ripped out the Dark's heart viciously. Blood coated his hand and halfway up his arm. The heart in his hand slowly stopped beating as he turned his attention to Ulrik.

"Looks like we have company." Ulrik's voice echoed throughout the warehouse.

He lifted his gaze to the shadows where Ulrik hid, the Dark's heart still in his hands. The body lay at his feet, and Asher flipped his hand over, dumping the heart as he stepped over the Fae.

His gaze was riveted on Ulrik, because unlike Rachel, he could see in the dark. Ulrik leaned against an iron beam with his arms crossed over his chest, his lips lifted in a smug grin.

"You were no' invited, Ash," Ulrik said.

He felt the Darks' blood running down his hands and dripping from his fingers as he drew closer to Rachel. He took his time getting to her. Ulrik was unpredictable, and he was much closer to Rachel than Asher, at the moment.

He could feel Rachel's eyes on him, could sense her relief. He didn't glance at her or tell her it was going to be all right. Because he wasn't sure if it would be.

As if Rachel knew not to move, she remained rooted to her spot as she followed his movements. Her purse fell from her shoulder and out of her fingers to drop onto the concrete.

"You dare to threaten Rachel and no' expect me to show?" he demanded.

Ulrik lifted a shoulder. "Did you fear she wasna telling you the truth? Is that why you had her followed?"

"I knew you would try something."

"Ah. Blaming it on me I see. No' a good start to this relationship."

He finally reached Rachel. She gripped his hand in both of hers. The coldness of her fingers and the way she shook with terror infuriated him.

"Your fight is with us. Leave the mortals out of it," Asher told him.

Ulrik snorted and straightened as he dropped his arms to his sides. "Leave them out of it? They're the ones who began this."

"No one ever denied that."

"No one wanted to do anything either."

Asher hated to admit it, but it was the truth. Their vow of protection prevented the Kings from any sort of retaliation then. Now, he wasn't sure what the Kings might do.

"You want someone to punish?" Asher asked. "I'm right here."

As he spoke, he subtly moved Rachel behind him, hoping to put more distance between her and Ulrik.

"Must we go through this every time I encounter one of you?" Ulrik asked, exasperated.

He shook his head as he lifted one shoulder in a shrug. "I doona know what you've told the others."

"Stop the bullshit."

He didn't smile when he heard the fury in Ulrik's words. He wasn't sure if it was better to have Ulrik calm and cold, or riled, because he was so capricious. He knew how precarious Rachel's position was. Ulrik brought her here to kill her. Asher didn't need to ask why. The why of it was evident.

"I'm going to win," Ulrik declared.

He shrugged. "Perhaps. Perhaps no'. That doesna give you the right to kill as you have."

"Just as none of you had the right to banish me from my home or force me to remain in this form," Ulrik coldly spat. "I would rather have been locked away with my Silvers than live like this."

"Everything you're doing is bringing the Kings closer than we've ever been. Each time you go after one of our women or attempt to reveal us to the mortals, you band us together. You're the one who is the outsider."

Ulrik's smile was taciturn. "Do you think Con would've given me back my magic or allowed me to return to the home I helped build if I'd been a good lad?"

"Maybe."

"Then you're a bigger fool than I ever thought you were. Con never had any such plans. He expected me to remain just as I was for eternity."

"You should've halted the killing when we asked."

Ulrik ignored his comment and asked, "If my actions brought such harsh justice, should they no' apply to all of us?"

He gave a nod, wondering what Ulrik was getting at. "Of course."

"Seems as if Con should turn some of that righteous justice on himself."

Ulrik's words caused him to frown. His implications were clear, and Asher didn't like where that led his thoughts. What did Ulrik know that the rest didn't? As close as they had once been, Ulrik would know all of Con's darkest secrets.

"What are you referring to?" he demanded, hoping to get more information.

Ulrik drew in a deep breath and slowly released it. "Ask Con."

There wasn't a need, and Ulrik knew it. Con didn't share anything with anyone. But there was Kellan. As Keeper of the History, he knew everything that happened with all of the Dragon Kings.

Ulrik suddenly smiled. "You've realized Kellan would know what I'm talking about. I wonder if he'd tell you."

"If it's so important, you tell me."

"And make it easy for Con? I doona think so."

Asher gave Rachel a little push, hoping she would make her way out of the warehouse. "If you really had something on Con, you wouldna hesitate to tell it."

"First," Ulrik said, his tone bored, "ask yourself why a brother would demand another to battle? I never gave Con any reason to think I wanted the position of King of Kings. He forced the issue. When I wouldna do as he ordered, he found another way to get rid of me."

Asher could only blink in shocked surprise. Ulrik placed the blame for everything that happened, from his lover betraying him to his banishment, on Con. It was true, the King of Kings could be ironfisted in his ruthless endeavor to protect them and Dreagan. He was a fierce, merciless bastard at times, but that's what came with wearing the mantle of King of Kings.

But now Ulrik had put doubt in Asher's mind.

It had been thousands of years ago, but he couldn't remember how Con learned of Ulrik's lover's betrayal. No matter how he searched his memory, there was nothing he could recall that would redeem—or condemn—Con.

He opened his mouth to ask another question, but Ulrik spoke over him.

"Second, it's a nice attempt to keep me talking about my favorite subject—the destruction of Con. However, Rachel willna get far."

Asher held Ulrik's gaze, trying to determine what his old friend was going to do. Out of the corner of his eye, he saw two Dark Fae materialize.

He turned to race after Rachel, but the Dark reached him first. Their hands grabbed him. Asher blinked, and he found himself in a chamber devoid of light with Dark all around him.

Chapter Sixteen

One minute Asher was there with two more of those ghastly Dark Fae, and the next he was gone. Rachel looked around, hoping to find some hint of him. But it was like he vanished.

The sound of something huge breathing behind her made her blood turn to ice. Panic enveloped Rachel in a cloak of dread and heart-pounding terror. One of those breaths blew her hair against her face. She squeezed her eyes closed, a cry falling from her lips as she began to shake uncontrollably.

She knew what was behind her. A dragon. Rather, Ulrik in dragon form.

This she hadn't prepared for. When Asher had arrived, she knew he would save the day and get them both out of there without anything happening. But she was once more alone. Except this time, she had no illusions of getting out alive.

Ulrik wanted her dead. Whether it was because she wasn't going to reveal the Kings to the world or because she'd fallen for Asher didn't matter. To Ulrik, they were one and the same. Both were punishable by death.

She waited to feel the pain of his bite, or even to hear his intake of breath right before he breathed fire. The longer she waited and nothing happened, the more anxious she became.

Rachel opened her eyes. Without moving her head, she looked to either side of her. There was no large talon or scales to be seen. Had she imagined the breath upon her neck and the sound of breathing?

It took several minutes listening to the noises of the building—and anything else—before she got the courage to turn around. She moved slowly, waiting for something to happen. Everything in the warehouse was quiet and still. Not even the pigeons were flying.

Before her was that same darkened area where Ulrik had taunted her. The shadows parted and a large head took shape, looming above her.

Her mouth fell open when she spied the silver scales covering the wide head of the dragon. She took in the slitted obsidian eyes that were trained on her and tried to scream, but no sound came out.

The head moved farther out of the darkness to reveal a row of dark silver tendrils at the base of his skull and disappearing into the shadows. More of those same dark silver tendrils surrounded his mouth, which parted to show her rows of very sharp white teeth.

She could swear he smiled, a growl rumbling through his chest.

Death was staring her right in the face.

And there was no escaping it.

Chapter Seventeen

Asher didn't bother to send out a message to the other Kings. No one could help him where he was now, and even if they tried, it would take too long for them to get there. The only way Rachel had a chance of survival was if he got back to her. And the only way to do that was use the Dark.

He counted eight in the chamber with him. How…ambitious…of them to think they could take him down with so small of numbers. Even without shifting to dragon form.

Without waiting for them to make the first move, he lunged to the side and plunged his hand into the chest of the Dark before yanking out his heart. He spun away as magic was thrown at him. He dodged most of the iridescent balls, but a few managed to land on him. The feel of the dark magic sinking through his skin into his bone was revolting.

And only pissed him off even more.

In two strides, he wrenched out the spinal columns of two Dark. As they fell dead at his feet, magic slammed into his right calf. He ignored it and moved toward the remaining five. They were clustered together, alternating throwing the bubbles of magic at him.

He gritted his teeth and ran toward them. The pain of the magic dimmed as he imagined what Ulrik was doing to Rachel. His gaze locked on a Dark and he effortlessly killed him. His gaze shifted to the left and he ended that Fae's life as well.

With each Dark that fell, he kept count. Until he had the last one pinned against the wall with his hand inside the Fae's chest, wrapped around his heart.

"If you doona want me ripping this out of your chest right this second, you'll return me to Paris and the warehouse where Ulrik is."

The Dark nodded woodenly. "Ta…take your hand off my heart."

Asher gave the muscle a hard squeeze, causing the Dark to wince. "That isna an option. On the count of three, you either take me or I pull me hand out. I'll still be holding your heart, though."

"If you kill me no one will take you back to Paris," the Dark said with a smile.

"If you doona, you'll be dead."

The cocky smile slipped from the Fae's face. "Taraeth will kill me."

"I doona give a shite what your king will do. I'm the one with the hand on your heart. One."

The Dark looked around frantically. "Wait. Please."

"Do you wait when a mortal asks you? Two."

"I...I," he stuttered with his hands flat against the wall and sweat rolling down his face. "I don't want to die."

"You know what to do. Thr-"

In the next instant, Asher was back at the warehouse. He heard the distinctive growl of a dragon and jerked his head to the side to see Ulrik looking down at Rachel.

Asher released the Dark, who immediately teleported away. Then he faced Ulrik. "You touch her, and I'll kill you."

Ulrik's head snapped up, a sound of outrage reverberating in his chest. Rachel shouted his name and hurried toward him. She tripped but managed to remain upright.

He didn't take his gaze from Ulrik. Quickly, Asher opened up the mental link and shouted, *"Ulrik can shift!"* to all the dragons.

Asher expected a response, but there was nothing. Until he heard laughter in his mind. Laughter he recognized.

"You should've stayed away," Ulrik said through the link.

"Asher," Rachel whispered.

He glanced at her. "Run. Hard and fast. Go straight to the airport and get to Dreagan. They're expecting you."

"I'm not leaving you."

He wanted to kiss her one last time, but if he didn't get her out now, she might not make it out at all. "You must."

"Afraid, Ash?" Ulrik goaded.

He was more afraid than he'd ever been. He wasn't scared of fighting Ulrik or even of dying. What terrified him was that Rachel wouldn't get away, that her life would end because of her connection to him.

Ulrik's eyes moved between him and Rachel. When Ulrik took a step toward them, Asher turned and placed a hard, quick kiss on her lips.

"Run," he whispered and gave her a push.

She took a few stumbling steps back before she turned and bolted. He then faced the dragon. If Ulrik wanted a fight, he was going to get one.

With merely a thought, Asher shifted. It went against everything Con demanded of the Kings, but he would deal with Con later. Right now he was more concerned with keeping Rachel alive long enough to get within the safety of Dreagan.

"Feels good, does it no'?" Ulrik asked.

Asher glared at him. *"You might've stopped my message getting to the Kings, but Rachel will tell them."*

"Maybe. If she makes it. It's such a verra long way to Dreagan. And no one will be waiting for her at the airport in Scotland."

With Ulrik somehow preventing Asher from talking to the other Kings, there was no way to alert anyone to what was going on. If Ulrik managed to kill him, there would be no one stopping him from ending Rachel's life as well.

And then none of the Kings would know that Ulrik was at full strength.

How long had all his magic been returned? Asher suspected from the very beginning. Ulrik had played them.

Again.

"You can shut up. I'm sick of hearing you talk."

Ulrik barked in laughter. *"Tired of hearing how I'm going to destroy your world?"*

"I'm tired of hearing how everyone should feel sorry for you. Shit happened. Get over it."

"Ah, but then you can say that since it didna happen to you."

"Would you feel better if I shed a tear?"

Ulrik released a roar loud enough to shatter what was left of the windows.

* * * *

Rachel was shaking so badly her legs wouldn't work right. She slipped and slid her way to the door. When she didn't hear Asher talking anymore, she glanced over her shoulder. And came to a jarring halt.

She'd wanted to know what he looked like in dragon form. Had wondered at the exact color of his scales. Now that she had an up-close-and-personal view, she was awed at the giants before her.

How naïve for her to think humans had a right to know of the Kings. Seeing the sheer size of them, the Dragon Kings could've ruled this world from the very beginning. They chose to hide instead.

She could only imagine what people would attempt to do to the Kings if the truth was known. They would be hunted until there was no choice but another war. No wonder the Kings went to such length to keep their secret.

Enthralled, she took a step toward Asher. She gaped at the thick, elongated body, and admired the hunter green scales that shaded nearly to black on his underbelly. Her gaze traveled down his body as she took in the thick, leathery wings folded against his body, to his long tail that curled toward him.

She took cautious, slow steps to the side to get a better look at him. With his words to "run" still echoing in her head, something warned her to stay. Even though it was dangerous to be so near two fighting dragons, setting off on her own where more Dark Fae—or humans—working for Ulrik could be waiting for her was pure folly.

Rachel bumped into a wall and put her back to it. She moved quietly along the way wishing she knew what they were saying. Just by seeing the way they tossed their heads, growled, or even smiled, there was a conversation going on.

Suddenly, Ulrik lifted his head and roared. She covered her ears against the sound. Glass shattered, raining down upon her so she had to curl in a ball, using her arms to cover her head.

When it finally stopped, she lifted her head just in time to see Ulrik jump from the shadows and slam into Asher. The two crashed to the ground, causing it to shake from the force, before they slid across the expanse of the warehouse crushing everything they came in contact with.

Not even the iron holding up the building was immune to the sheer might and power of the dragons. Several pillars dented, creaking and groaning, each time one of the dragons crashed into one. To her shock, one, then two pillars broke in half.

She looked up, wondering if the warehouse would be able to withstand the battle. For now, that was the only thing hiding Asher and Ulrik, but if it came down, everything the Dragon Kings had done to hide would be for naught.

When she glanced back at the dragons, she realized their battle had brought them closer to her. Asher stretched out one of his wings and turned, slamming it against the side of Ulrik's head.

Ulrik let out a grunt as he fell, sliding right toward her.

She screeched, but the sound was drowned out by Ulrik's talons scrapping against the concrete as he scrambled to his feet. Then he charged Asher.

She looked from side to side, wondering where the safest place was. And there wasn't one. She remained huddled against the wall, raising her arm to block her head and face any time she spotted an object coming her way.

The more she watched, the more she was amazed the Dragon Kings had been able to keep their secret from getting out. How did anyone miss such a huge beast in the night sky?

She winced when Ulrik got in a few goods hits on Asher. With each one, her worry grew as she recalled that the only way a Dragon King could be killed was by another King. The thought of losing Asher after just finding him sent a wave of anguish through her so fierce she felt it go right into her soul.

He was fighting for her, to protect her. And he might die because of her. How was she ever going to live with that? There was no way she could.

She had no idea how much time passed before Asher and Ulrik broke apart, circling each other. Her legs were cramping from squatting for such a long period. She bit her lip from the pain as she stood.

Her feet were numb, the feeling rushing back to them like a thousand pinpricks. She gasped when Ulrik's tail came within inches of hitting her as he passed. One swipe of that tail and she would be history. She looked toward the door. Whatever opening had been there was long gone. Even if she wanted to leave, she couldn't.

Asher released a low, rumbling growl and they were once more locked in battle. Ulrik bit down on Asher's neck sending blood running down his dark green scales.

He and Ulrik battled to get the upper hand. Asher was just about to win when Ulrik slashed his talons along the bite wound. He lost his grip, and Ulrik pushed him away.

She didn't move as Asher fell, sliding right to her. His head was ten feet from her. For a second he didn't move. Then he opened his eyes. She found herself staring into almond-shaped alabaster eyes.

She knew the instant it registered that she was there. He blinked and rose, putting himself between her and Ulrik. Because if he had seen her, then it was only a matter of time before Ulrik did.

Her heart thudded painfully in her chest. Each second felt like an eternity. Every hit, every bite, every wound Ulrik inflicted on Asher, she felt.

And every time he hurt Ulrik, she silently cheered.

She began to relax when it appeared that Asher was winning. Ulrik missed more than he landed any hits. While Asher had made sure to keep himself between them, he drew closer to Ulrik to win the battle.

Though Asher wasn't near, she wasn't worried. He would defeat Ulrik and end this awful day on a high note. But all that changed when Ulrik pinned him down in a blink. When Ulrik's obsidian eyes locked on her, she realized it had all been a trick to get Asher away from her.

Ulrik drew in a deep breath, his chest expanding. She knew this was the end. Her vision clouded as tears filled her eyes before falling down her cheeks. She looked to Asher.

Right before Ulrik breathed fire, Asher punched him under the chin, knocking his head back and sending the fire straight up. Asher then got free and rushed to her. She squeezed her eyes closed as she waited for his large dragon body to slam into her. Instead, she felt a gust of wind. She opened her eyes in time to see him surround her body with his wings.

A half a second before fire rained down on them. Not even Asher's scales or wings could halt the heat that scorched her, billowing her hair and causing her to break out into an instant sweat.

It became difficult to breathe.

And then she stopped trying.

Chapter Eighteen

Asher waited for Ulrik to strike again. He couldn't move for fear Ulrik would breathe dragon fire again and it reach Rachel. Seconds ticked by with no sound. He lifted his head and looked around, his dragon eyes penetrating shadows. But there was no sign of Ulrik.

He pulled his wings around and tucked them against him as he lowered his gaze to Rachel and spotted her lying limply within his hands. His heart caught, anguish ripping through him when he spotted the heat burns.

Shifting back to human form, he held her tightly against him with one arm while he felt her pulse with the other. She breathed—barely. Her hair was plastered to her head as beads of sweat ran down her face. Her clothes were soaked as well. She couldn't remain in those clothes for long with the frigid temperatures.

"Rae, open your eyes," he urged as he caressed his fingers along her cheek. "Look at me, *a ghràidh*."

He'd protected her from the fire. He knew it hadn't reached her. But he hadn't been able to stop the heat. Dragon fire was the hottest thing on the realm. Nothing could withstand it but a dragon.

Was it Fate that sent him to Paris and in Rachel's path? It must be because his power was healing burns from dragon fire. He pushed his magic down his arm and through his hand into her. A shaking sigh left him when he saw her burns begin to heal.

The sound of metal moving on his left had him jerking up his head. He was prepared to shift back into a dragon to protect his woman and continue fighting Ulrik. But as the sunlight pierced the darkness, he was surprised to see Blossom Engel daintily step over debris and enter the warehouse.

She folded her hands before her and didn't so much as bat an eye.

"Sir, I believe we should leave. The sounds of the battle were heard and the authorities called. We also need to get Ms. Marek out of those clothes—and you into some."

Without a doubt, she knew what he was. He wasn't sure how to feel about it. At the moment, he was thankful. The rest, well, he'd deal with that later.

Still, he hesitated. Ulrik could be anywhere. Then his gaze narrowed on Ms. Engel. Con would never have told her their secret, nor would he have allowed her to see anything. That meant someone had told her. And that someone must be Ulrik.

She took another step toward Asher. "I know what you're thinking, but I'd never betray you, Con, or anyone at Dreagan."

"How can I believe you?"

"You have to trust me."

He looked down at Rachel. She needed to be tended to, and he couldn't exactly walk around Paris naked carrying her back to the hotel. Gathering Rachel in his arms, he got to his feet and made his way to Ms. Engel until he stood even with her. Then he said, "If I find out you've betrayed us in any way, I'll kill you myself."

"I would expect nothing less." She then turned on her heel and strode out of the ruins.

Asher followed her outside. His gaze swept the area, and despite him telling her and the men she hired to leave, they had remained. He halted as he counted all four. They were hidden so well that a mortal would never have been able to see them. But he wasn't a mere human.

Ms. Engel reached the opened door of the car. She turned to the side and saw he'd stopped. Without asking why, she simply said, "Your secret has never been in safer hands."

"I'm supposed to trust you on this?"

"You are. My group has a number of secrets that will never pass their lips."

He couldn't take that chance, but he'd have to return to find them. Right now he had to get Rachel to safety. As he climbed into the car, something caught his attention out of the corner of his eye.

He saw a man in a dark suit with long black hair walking away. Ulrik.

"Rachel needs you," Ms. Engel said from inside the car.

Asher hesitated but remained in the car. No sooner had the door closed than Ms. Engel shoved his hands away from Rachel. He could only watch as the car drove away and Blossom began to hurriedly undress Rachel until she was in nothing but her underwear.

Ms. Engel threw a blanket over her that he tucked around Rachel. The longer it went on without Rachel stirring, the more worried he became.

"There were two men."

He frowned as he turned his head to Ms. Engel. "I'm sorry?"

"The one you fought left before I entered the building. The other watched it all."

Watched? He frowned as he tried to figure out who it could be. "Did you see his face?"

"I didn't get close enough. We remained hidden until the fighting was over."

He saw them pass the street they needed to take to get back to the hotel. "Where are we going?"

"To the airport where a plane awaits to return you to Dreagan. I called ahead to have them on standby."

He wanted to trust her, but Ulrik had shown how easily it was to integrate someone into their lives. She was helping now, but when would that change?

"There will be clothes waiting for you on the plane," she continued. "I'll also have both of your suites packed and everything sent to Dreagan immediately."

"Why no' come with me?" he asked. Then he and Con could talk to her together.

She gave him a kind smile. "I'd like nothing more than to visit, however Dreagan needs a representative here to finish the WWC. And that reminds me, Dreagan won both votes, as usual. I'm loath to say that Glenfiddich continues to gain ground with the judges and the popular vote."

"Dreagan has been on top for many years. People get tired of the same ones winning all the time. It's good for both Glenfiddich and us to have that competition."

"There is no competition when you look at the sales."

He nodded as he ran a hand over Rachel's wet hair. "And that's what matters in the end."

There was no more talk until they reached the airfield. Just as Ms. Engel had said, the same plane that brought him to Paris was ready and waiting.

The car pulled on to the back side of the plane where the door was and stopped. Asher turned to Ms. Engel. "How do you know about me?"

"Not in the way you think."

"Then tell me."

She smiled as the driver opened the car door. "Take care of Ms. Marek."

He wanted to remain and get the truth from Ms. Engel, but once more he was reminded of what really mattered to him—Rachel. He got out of the car and strode naked to the steps of the plane.

No sooner was he inside than the door was closed and the plane began taxiing down the runway. He lay Rachel down on a sofa and put on the jeans, boots, and white tee shirt he found folded on a seat.

By the time he finished, they were already in the air and returning to Dreagan. The entire way back, he went over everything in his mind, attempting to sort it all out, but the more he thought he figured out, the more tangled things became.

When they reached Inverness, he picked Rachel up and departed the plane to find Lily sitting in the pilot's seat of her helicopter with the blades turning. Her smile fell when she noticed Rachel in his arms. Asher carefully climbed into the chopper, still holding her. Once he was seated, he put on the earphones.

"Is she hurt?" Lily asked, her gaze on Rachel.

"I fought Ulrik to keep him from killing her."

Lily didn't ask more as they became airborne. The flight was quick and smooth, but it was the longest trip of his life because Rachel wouldn't open her eyes.

As soon as Dreagan came into view, he wanted to jump from the chopper and shift to fly Rachel home, as he should be able to. He saw the manor and the mountain connected to their home. Behind the mountain was a secret entrance for the Kings to enter when in dragon form.

So much of their lives had been altered and continued to change. They could blame it on Ulrik, but he shouldn't shoulder the culpability alone. Each of them was responsible.

As soon as they landed, Lily shut down the blades. He removed the earphones and gathered Rachel in his arms. The door opened and Anson stood staring at Rachel.

He climbed from the chopper and strode toward the manner, ignoring the MI5 agents who tried to get a look at him. It was difficult since Dragon Kings he hadn't known were there surrounded him, making it impossible for anyone to see what he carried.

"It's time those fuckers left," Roman stated angrily.

Asher agreed. MI5 had been on the estate long enough without finding anything. It was time something be done.

"It's being handled," Vaughn replied.

Vaughn was acting attorney for Dreagan, and nothing stood in the way of him when he set his sights on something. MI5 would be gone soon, but the world's attention on Dreagan wouldn't lessen for a long time.

"What happened?" Anson asked.

"Ulrik." He entered the manor and halted in the solarium when he spotted Con.

Con closed the distance between them and looked down at Rachel. "Is she wounded?"

"I healed her."

At this, Con's brow furrowed as concern flashed in his black eyes. "See to Rachel."

"Then we need to talk."

Con gave a nod and stepped aside. Asher made his way up the stairs to his chamber on the third floor. He laid Rachel on his bed, covering her with the blankets. He knelt by the bed and smoothed a lock of dark hair from her face.

"Doona sleep long," he whispered and placed a kiss on her lips.

Then he got to his feet and walked to the door. As he stepped into the wide hallway, he saw Lily and Grace waiting for him.

"We'll watch over her," Lily said.

Grace nodded. "All the mates will take turns until she wakes."

He bowed his head. "Thank you."

"Con's waiting in his office," Lily said.

With one last look at the door, Asher walked to the stairs and descended to the second floor. Several Kings were already standing outside Con's door when he arrived.

He gave a nod to Anson before entering the office. Con sat behind his large desk in his customary dress shirt and gold dragon-head cuff links. Against the wall to the left, Rhys and Kiril stood together, and a few feet away were Warrick and Thorn. Sitting in one of the chairs before Con's desk was Kellan.

"Have a seat," Con bade Asher, pointing to the chair beside Kellan.

He was too emotional to sit. Instead, he remained by the door. Con's office was large, but with so many Kings in attendance, it became crowded quickly.

"What happened?" Rhys asked into the silence.

He looked at Kellan, who already knew everything, and most likely had already written it down as Keeper of the Hisory. But Kellan simply returned his look, waiting. Asher then took a deep breath and began the story. No one spoke as he talked about meeting Rachel or how suspicious Ms. Engel was of her. The silence continued as he explained how Ulrik had gotten to Rachel, using her for his own motives.

The fury was palpable when he told them of his exchange with Ulrik and subsequent battle.

"Your quick thinking saved Rachel," Kellan said.

Kiril shook his head in shock. "I knew he'd gotten his magic back. But why wait until now to shift?"

"Why bring Lily back from the dead only to attempt to kill Darcy and now Rachel?" Rhys asked.

"Why hasn't he woken his Silvers?" Thorn asked.

Asher shrugged. "I doona know any answers. All I know is what we experienced."

"But you doona know what he said to Rachel," Con stated.

"As soon as she wakes I intend to find out."

Warrick crossed his arms over his chest. "I'm sure it was the usual threats and such."

"More so since he put her on the job," Thorn added.

Asher couldn't stop thinking of the insinuation Ulrik made against Con. The Kings had been divided once, and it took Con to pull them back together. If he said something now, in front of everyone, it could break apart the slim threads that held them together. Especially if Ulrik was wrong.

All it took was just a whisper of doubt to destroy everything the Kings were. It was exactly what Ulrik wanted, the very thing he threatened Con that he'd do.

He slid his gaze to Kellan to find him staring. Kellan never gave anything away. Asher couldn't imagine the secrets he kept, and he never took sides, always keeping everything to himself.

Thinking it better to wait until he could get Con alone, he moved on to another topic. "Tell me of Ms. Engel."

Con raised a blond brow, his eyes showing no emotion. "She's been my assistant each time I go to the WWC. She's amazing at what she does."

"Without question," Asher said. "I'm curious at how she knows what we are."

Con slowly sat up from his chair. "She doesna."

"Actually, she does."

Chapter Nineteen

Rachel opened her eyes. It wasn't torn or twisted metal that met her gaze but pristine white crown molding thick enough to make the queen of England envious.

She couldn't remember why the anxiousness and terror filled her, but she knew it was important. She tried to sort through her memories to find the source of such emotions, and the longer she went without discovering it, the more distressed she became.

Something…no, *someone* was important to her.

"You're awake."

The English accent startled her. Rachel turned her head to find a beautiful woman with long ebony hair, kind black eyes, and a welcoming smile.

"I'm Lily," she said. She motioned with her thumb beside her. "And this is Grace."

Rachel's gaze slid to the side to find another woman of uncommon beauty with short blond hair and eyes so dark a blue they were almost black.

"Hi," Grace said with a wave of her fingers. "We've been worried."

American. Rachel frowned as she looked at the dark gray walls. Where was she? As soon as her gaze met a large painting of a hunter green dragon with a horde of hunter green dragons behind him, she knew.

She was at Dreagan.

That meant Asher had won. She closed her eyes and smiled. Now she understood those horrid emotions when she woke. It felt so good to be able to let them go.

"How do you feel?" Lily asked as she rose from her seat to stand by the bed.

She licked her lips and took stock of her body. "I feel…fine."

But she hadn't earlier. That part she remembered clear as day.

"That's Asher's doing," Grace said. "His power is to heal burns from dragon fire."

Rachel slowly pushed herself up to lean against the headboard. She pulled the deep green silk sheets up under her armpits and nodded, at a loss for words. She shoved her hair over her shoulder and winced. It felt grimy from sweat.

"I'm sure you want some time alone," Grace said.

Lily backed up her petite frame. "Of course. Forgive us. The bathroom is there," she said, pointing to a cracked door to the left. "Your bags were delivered a few minutes ago, so you should have everything you need."

"You can wait here for Asher if you want," Grace said. "He'll be looking for you once he's done with the other Kings. Or you can turn right in the hallway and make your way downstairs where we'll be."

Lily walked to the door and opened it. Once Grace was through, she turned her head to Rachel and said, "We can show you around. I'm sure you have lots of questions, and there's no telling how long the guys will be locked in Con's office."

With that, Lily closed the door behind her. Rachel released a breath. She was at Dreagan. Asher had told her he'd bring her, but she supposed she hadn't really believed it would happen.

She threw off the covers and looked down at her body. Everything was where it should be, which was more than she had thought was possible before she passed out. She swung her legs over the bed and hesitantly got to her feet, amazed that she felt better than she had in a long time. She wasn't tired or aching or anything.

That's what magic could do. She shook her head with a smile and walked to her luggage to grab her toiletry bag and some clothes before she headed into the shower.

* * * *

"What the hell do you mean 'she knows'?" Kiril demanded.

Asher shot him a hard look. "What do you think I mean? Somehow, Blossom Engel, assistant extraordinaire, knows we're Dragon Kings."

"She actually said that?" Con asked.

He shook his head. "Remember when I told you she was with me as we drove to the warehouse? I ordered her to leave and to take the men she hired to watch Rachel. But they didna."

Con's gaze swung to Kellan. "Why did you no' tell me?"

"Perhaps because I do my best to forget whatever I see after I record it," Kellan replied crossly.

Asher continued. "Ms. Engel walked in, not at all perturbed to find me in the buff or to see the warehouse torn to shreds. She didna see anything, but she heard enough."

"And the men she hired?" War asked.

"The same. She said they kept secrets for a living. I had a suspicion that Ulrik might've used her as he did Rachel."

Kiril raised a brow, his shamrock green eyes locked on Asher. "Had? Or have?"

"I'm no' sure," he admitted. "She wouldna answer how she knew, but she does."

Con sat back in his chair and steepled his fingers. "We need to know. I had Ryder do a thorough background check on her years ago, and he does one each year before the WWC."

Ryder's background checks meant he looked under every stone, opened every closet for skeletons to find anything and everything on a person. No one did background checks like Ryder—not even any of the governments.

"And the men," Kellan pointed out.

Con gave a nod. "Aye. Those men as well."

There was a beat of silence before Rhys asked angrily, "Why has no one said shite about Ulrik being able to shift?"

"Because I think we all half expected it," Kiril replied.

Asher watched Con. He gave nothing away in his actions or facial expressions, but the way he controlled himself was also a tell. Con might not have known Ulrik could shift, but he'd suspected.

And Asher wasn't the only one to notice.

"You knew," Thorn stated, his gaze narrowed on Con.

Con looked at Thorn and held his gaze. With a snort, Thorn walked from the office, the others making way for him. A moment later, War followed.

"You should've told us," Anson stated.

Con's black eyes slid to Anson. "What would that have accomplished?"

"It could've prepared Asher."

Con dropped his hands to his stomach, his gaze narrowing. "Ever since we discovered it was Ulrik behind everything, I've warned each of you to expect anything, to be prepared for anything."

"I'm tired of Ulrik continuing to surprise us," Rhys said. "No matter what we do, he's at least one step ahead."

Asher looked at each of them. "I think that's because there's a spy at Dreagan."

Despite everything he'd relayed since returning to Dreagan, it was this statement that caused the office to grow so quiet you could hear a pin drop.

"I've begun to think that as well," Roman said from behind him.

Kellan dropped his foot to the ground and leaned forward, with his elbows on the arms of the chair. "It's a logical deduction based on how Ulrik always knows what we're doing. But I doona like thinking it's one of us."

"There's no other explanation," Kiril said.

"This will have to wait. We've some people missing."

Asher frowned as he looked around the room. "Who?"

"I sent Dmitri to check out whether a skeleton that has been found is a dragon," Con announced.

Asher's eyes widened. "We destroyed all of them."

"We thought we did," Kellan replied.

"And the others?"

"Kinsey, Esther, and Henry are on a mission. After what Kyvor did to Kinsey and Esther, they have a plan to return to see what they can find," Con explained.

Asher couldn't believe Ryder had let Kinsey go without him.

Rhys dropped his arms and pushed away from the wall. "You need to call a meeting, Con. Everyone needs to know these latest updates on Ulrik and the potential spy."

"Nay," Con stated as he got to his feet in one fluid motion. "I doona want anyone speaking of a spy outside of this office. Ulrik wants us to turn on each other. I'll no' give him the ammunition to do it."

Kiril ran a hand through his wheat-colored hair as he held Con's gaze. "I believe it's too late for that. We need to find the spy."

"I'll start immediately," Kellan said. "Asher, I'd like your help."

One by one, everyone left Con's office but Asher, Kellan, and Con. When the last King was out the door, Asher closed it and leaned back against it.

"I assume you have something on your mind," Con said. "By the way you and Kellan have been sharing looks, I gather this has to do with Ulrik and something he said."

Asher came around the chair and sat next to Kellan. "You know?"

"It's no' the first time Ulrik has tried to turn a King against me," Con confided.

He hadn't considered that, but he should've. If Ulrik would say such things to him, why wouldn't he say it to other Kings?

"What did he say?" Con asked.

Asher took a deep breath and released it. "He said that if a King should be punished, then you should turn that punishment on yourself."

"Did he say why?"

"He told me to ask you."

Kellan sat back in his chair without saying a word.

Asher looked from Kellan to Con, but Con kept his gaze locked on Asher. That's when he knew there was some truth to what Ulrik said. Getting it out of Con or Kellan, however, was going to be impossible.

And perhaps that was for the best. Right now the Kings needed to stay together. If they fractured apart, then Ulrik would win and the war with the mortals would start back up again.

Except this time the humans had nuclear bombs they wouldn't hesitate to use in an attempt to kill off the Dragon Kings. It wouldn't harm them, but it would devastate the land and any mortal within distance.

He didn't want that. He thought he'd wanted the truth. Now he wished he hadn't said anything to Con. Eventually the truth would come out. If Con was smart, he'd tell everyone now and not let Ulrik have that ammunition.

Then again, Con was the most stubborn of them all. He wouldn't tell anyone anything.

Asher pushed to his feet. "I'm going to check on Rachel."

"Is she your mate?" Con asked.

He looked Con in the eye and said, "Without a doubt."

Chapter Twenty

Rachel was about to step out of the shower when the door opened. Through the steam, she saw a face that made her smile. Asher's grin was large as he stepped into the water in his clothes.

His arms came around her as he lifted her off her feet, nuzzling her neck.

"You're still dressed," Rachel said with a laugh.

"I couldna wait." He set her down and smoothed her hair from her face. "How do you feel?"

"Good. I'd feel even better if you were out of those clothes," she said with a wink.

In record time he removed his clothes and closed the shower door. As he drew her back into his arms, Rachel knew this was where she wanted to be. She rested her head on his chest with the water hitting her back and closed her eyes.

"What are you thinking?"

She grinned, because she'd been wondering the same thing. "I thought I was going to die in that warehouse."

"I told you to leave for that verra reason."

"I couldn't leave you."

"Even if it meant your death?"

She nodded and opened her eyes to stare at the tile. "Even then. But you saved me."

"Barely."

"You still saved me."

His gaze slid away briefly. "You saw me in my true form."

At this she smiled. "Yes, and you were magnificent."

"You weren't afraid."

"Not of you. Never of you." That was the truth from the very beginning. Her heart had realized it. It had just taken her brain a little longer to catch up. She lifted her head and looked into his green eyes. "I know this may seem too soon since we've only just met, but I think I'm in love with you."

One dark brow lifted as his lips curled in a smile. "You *think?*"

"I know that in your arms is where I want to be. I know that the thought of waking up without you terrifies me. I know that with you, I feel whole. As if you were a missing piece that I didn't even know I needed. I've never been in love before. The only people I ever told 'I love you' was my family."

"We are your family now. You'll never be alone, Rae."

"Even after what I did with Ulrik?"

He gave a nod. "I explained the situation."

"Good." She wanted to rejoice, but she couldn't. It wasn't like she expected him to say he loved her—but she had hoped.

"Rae?"

"Hmm?" she asked as she stared at his chest.

"I have a confession."

She ran her hand over his dragon tattoo on his arm. As she did, she frowned, because she was sure the tat moved.

"I love you."

It took a second for his words to penetrate. Her gaze snapped to his face. "What?"

"I love you."

She knew she was smiling like an idiot, but she couldn't help it. "You do?"

"Aye, *a ghràidh.*"

"What does that mean?"

"'My love.'"

Her lips parted in awe as she realized he said that the first time they'd made love.

"I've loved you since then," he confessed.

She threw her arms around him and buried her face in his neck. "I love you. I love you. IloveyouIloveyouIloveyou."

He laughed and squeezed her tight. "I want you to be mine. Forever."

That's when the reality hit her. Her happiness faded as she pulled out of his arms. "There can't be a forever for us. I'm mortal."

"Did I no' tell you?" he said with a grin. "When a Dragon King and mortal take binding vows as mates, that mortal becomes *im*mortal. The only way the mate will die is if the King is killed."

Immortality. It was mindboggling, but then again, everything to do with Asher's world was magical. Why should this be any different? To be with him forever. It felt...right. "Then we really can have eternity?"

"Aye, *a ghràidh.*"

"There's no other place I'd rather be than by your side."

His smile wasn't nearly as bright as she'd hoped. "There's more. No child has been born alive between a King and a human. Most women miscarry within weeks. The verra few who carry the child to term give birth to a stillborn. Children willna be a part of our future."

"I have you. That's all I need." Those weren't just words. She'd known for a long time that with her job, children didn't fit. Hell, a boyfriend hadn't fit. Things were different with Asher, but that didn't mean her biological clock was ticking. In fact, that clock had never worked, and she was just fine with that.

Besides, the Kings had too many enemies at the moment for her to want to bring a child into the mix.

He looked into her eyes for a long minute before he yanked her against him and savagely kissed her. Instantly, her body ignited. She sank into the kiss, happier than she thought possible.

She had her Dragon King and the desire she hadn't thought she'd ever experience. No matter what, her cup runneth over.

Epilogue

Alone in his office, Con stood staring out his window. His worst fear had come to fruition. Ulrik could shift. He'd suspected it for a while. What he didn't understand was why Ulrik hadn't shifted when they fought.

There was a reason. Everything Ulrik did was for a reason. Just as he didn't shift when they fought, Ulrik did it now for a specific purpose. The fact that he didn't know what Ulrik was up to sent a thread of unease down his back.

His gaze was on his desk, but he didn't see the reports or papers. He saw Ulrik's face. His once best friend was single-handedly destroying everything he'd worked so hard to preserve.

Just as Ulrik had warned eons ago, Con's past was catching up with him. He never expected it would be Ulrik who led the charge against him, however.

If only that were the end to his problems. He now had to deal with a spy. He knew exactly how easily the Kings could take sides. They'd done it once before, fracturing them as they chose either him or Ulrik.

That couldn't happen again.

It *wouldn't* happen again.

Kellan might be looking into the spy, but he would do his own investigating. Because if it was another Dragon King putting everyone at Dreagan in danger, he wouldn't hesitate to banish a King again.

The only thing that mattered was Dreagan and the continuation of the Dragon Kings. And it all rested heavily on Con's shoulders.

* * * *

Also from 1001 Dark Nights and Donna Grant, discover Dragon King.

Sign up for the 1001 Dark Nights Newsletter
and be entered to win a Tiffany Key necklace.

There's a contest every month!

Go to www.1001DarkNights.com to subscribe.

As a bonus, all subscribers will receive a free
1001 Dark Nights story
The First Night
by Lexi Blake & M.J. Rose

Turn the page for a full list of the
1001 Dark Nights fabulous novellas...

Discover 1001 Dark Nights Collection Three

HIDDEN INK by Carrie Ann Ryan
A Montgomery Ink Novella

BLOOD ON THE BAYOU by Heather Graham
A Cafferty & Quinn Novella

SEARCHING FOR MINE by Jennifer Probst
A Searching For Novella

DANCE OF DESIRE by Christopher Rice

ROUGH RHYTHM by Tessa Bailey
A Made In Jersey Novella

DEVOTED by Lexi Blake
A Masters and Mercenaries Novella

Z by Larissa Ione
A Demonica Underworld Novella

FALLING UNDER YOU by Laurelin Paige
A Fixed Trilogy Novella

EASY FOR KEEPS by Kristen Proby
A Boudreaux Novella

UNCHAINED by Elisabeth Naughton
An Eternal Guardians Novella

HARD TO SERVE by Laura Kaye
A Hard Ink Novella

DRAGON FEVER by Donna Grant
A Dark Kings Novella

KAYDEN/SIMON by Alexandra Ivy/Laura Wright
A Bayou Heat Novella

STRUNG UP by Lorelei James
A Blacktop Cowboys® Novella

MIDNIGHT UNTAMED by Lara Adrian
A Midnight Breed Novella

TRICKED by Rebecca Zanetti
A Dark Protectors Novella

DIRTY WICKED by Shayla Black
A Wicked Lovers Novella

A SEDUCTIVE INVITATION by Lauren Blakely
A Seductive Nights New York Novella

SWEET SURRENDER by Liliana Hart
A MacKenzie Family Novella

For more information, visit www.1001DarkNights.com.

Discover 1001 Dark Nights Collection One

FOREVER WICKED by Shayla Black
CRIMSON TWILIGHT by Heather Graham
CAPTURED IN SURRENDER by Liliana Hart
SILENT BITE: A SCANGUARDS WEDDING by Tina
Folsom
DUNGEON GAMES by Lexi Blake
AZAGOTH by Larissa Ione
NEED YOU NOW by Lisa Renee Jones
SHOW ME, BABY by Cherise Sinclair
ROPED IN by Lorelei James
TEMPTED BY MIDNIGHT by Lara Adrian
THE FLAME by Christopher Rice
CARESS OF DARKNESS by Julie Kenner

Also from 1001 Dark Nights

TAME ME by J. Kenner

For more information, visit www.1001DarkNights.com.

Discover 1001 Dark Nights Collection Two

WICKED WOLF by Carrie Ann Ryan
WHEN IRISH EYES ARE HAUNTING by Heather Graham
EASY WITH YOU by Kristen Proby
MASTER OF FREEDOM by Cherise Sinclair
CARESS OF PLEASURE by Julie Kenner
ADORED by Lexi Blake
HADES by Larissa Ione
RAVAGED by Elisabeth Naughton
DREAM OF YOU by Jennifer L. Armentrout
STRIPPED DOWN by Lorelei James
RAGE/KILLIAN by Alexandra Ivy/Laura Wright
DRAGON KING by Donna Grant
PURE WICKED by Shayla Black
HARD AS STEEL by Laura Kaye
STROKE OF MIDNIGHT by Lara Adrian
ALL HALLOWS EVE by Heather Graham
KISS THE FLAME by Christopher Rice
DARING HER LOVE by Melissa Foster
TEASED by Rebecca Zanetti
THE PROMISE OF SURRENDER by Liliana Hart

Also from 1001 Dark Nights

THE SURRENDER GATE By Christopher Rice
SERVICING THE TARGET By Cherise Sinclair

For more information, visit www.1001DarkNights.com.

About Donna Grant

New York Times and USA Today bestselling author Donna Grant has been praised for her "totally addictive" and "unique and sensual" stories. She's the author of more than thirty novels spanning multiple genres of romance. Her latest acclaimed series, Dark Kings, features dragons, the Fae, and immortal Highlanders who are dark, dangerous, and irresistible.

She lives with her two children, three dogs, and four cats in Texas.

For more information about Donna, visit her website at www.DonnaGrant.com.

The Hero
Sons of Texas, Book 1
By Donna Grant
Coming December 6, 2016

Owen Loughman is a highly-decorated Navy SEAL who has a thirst for action. But there's one thing he hasn't been able to forget: his high school sweetheart, Natalie. After more than a decade away, Owen has returned home to the ranch in Texas for a dangerous new mission that puts him face-to-face with Natalie and an outside menace that threatens everything he holds dear. He'll risk it all to keep Natalie safe—and win her heart.

Natalie Dixon has had a lifetime of heartache since Owen was deployed. Fourteen years and one bad marriage later, she finds herself mixed up with the Loughmans again. With her life on the line against an enemy she can't fight alone, it's Owen's strong shoulders, smoldering eyes, and sensuous smile that she turns to. When danger closes in, how much will she risk to stay with the only man she's ever loved?

* * * *

Natalie didn't see the black fence that lined either side of the drive, or the cows and horses that grazed peacefully.

Her gaze was locked on the white house that drew closer with each second. By the time she parked in front of the two-story ranch home with its wide, wrap-around porch, all she could think about was the dinner she'd had the week before with Callie, Virgil, and Charlotte.

She put the car in park and glanced around. There was no sign that anyone else was there. Since she expected someone to come out at the sound of her car, she assumed Owen and his brothers hadn't yet made it to the house.

Or perhaps, luck was on her side, and those choppers hadn't been bringing the brothers.

She got out of her car, but it was more difficult than she imagined making herself go up the steps to the porch. She might be involved in all of this, but she'd never witnessed a murder scene firsthand.

Frankly, she didn't want to.

But Orrin's life was on the line. Everything she and Callie could discover only helped their chances of learning who took Orrin and where Ragnarok was.

She reached the front door. At least she wouldn't have to see Virgil's and Charlotte's bodies. They had already been taken away.

That was her last thought as she walked through the doorway and found herself flat on her back. Natalie knew the instant the large hands grabbed her that it was Owen.

Her heart skipped a beat, even as she instinctively reacted and used her momentum to pull Owen over her head. She got up, but in the next heartbeat, he had her pinned to the wall.

The heat of him was the first thing she felt. Then it was his hard body trapping her. She felt herself softening, needing to feel him after all these years.

She thought he would threaten her. Instead, he knocked off her cap. His dark brown eyes widened in shock.

How she wished her heart didn't feel like it was about to explode out of her chest. He was . . . breathtaking. She drank in the very sight of him. Sharp, chiseled features that looked as if they had been fashioned from granite stared back at her. Gone was any hint of the teenager she'd known. Before her stood a man in all his masculine glory.

He'd always been tall, his muscles honed at an early age from working on the ranch. Now, however, Owen filled out his wide shoulders. His light tan tee stretched tightly across his chest, molding to every ripple of muscle in his arms and shoulders. The shirt was tucked into camo pants she imagined were for the desert by their sand and khaki color. His hair was longer, the dark strands shoved away from his face in long waves.

Her surprise at having Owen against her was quickly hidden. Out of the corner of her eye, she spotted two more figures. How she wished she would've waited for Callie.

"Hi, boys," Natalie said. It was the only thing she could think of.

Owen frowned, the irritation clear in his sensual chocolate gaze. "What the hell are you doing here?"

Discover More Donna Grant

Dragon King
A Dark Kings Novella

A Woman On A Mission

Grace Clark has always done things safe. She's never colored outside of the law, but she has a book due and has found the perfect spot to break through her writer's block. Or so she thinks. Right up until Arian suddenly appears and tries to force her away from the mountain. Unaware of the war she just stumbled into, Grace doesn't just discover the perfect place to write, she finds Arian - the most gorgeous, enticing, mysterious man she's ever met.

A King With a Purpose

Arian is a Dragon King who has slept away centuries in his cave. Recently woken, he's about to leave his mountain to join his brethren in a war when he's alerted that someone has crossed onto Dreagan. He's ready to fight...until he sees the woman. She's innocent and mortal - and she sets his blood aflame. He recognizes the danger approaching her just as the dragon within him demands he claim her for his own...

On behalf of 1001 Dark Nights,

Liz Berry and M.J. Rose would like to thank ~

Steve Berry
Doug Scofield
Kim Guidroz
Jillian Stein
InkSlinger PR
Dan Slater
Asha Hossain
Chris Graham
Pamela Jamison
Jessica Johns
Dylan Stockton
Richard Blake
BookTrib After Dark
The Dinner Party Show
and Simon Lipskar

Made in the USA
Lexington, KY
22 September 2016